THE BARFLY

&

OTHER ODDITIES

BIG JOHN MCKENZIE

This book is a work of fiction. All characters, incidents, and dialogue, except for incidental references to public figures, products, or services, are fictional and are not intended to disparage any person, living or dead, or any company or company's products and services.

ISBN 13 978-1-7330743-2-2 (Hardcover)

ISBN 13 978-1-7330743-3-9 (Paperback)

McKenzie, John R.
The Barfly and Other Oddities/ Big John McKenzie

Cover art by Dragan Bilic at Upwork.com

This book is a gift from the Muse of Imagination
and is hereby dedicated in her gracious honor.

Author's Note:

Often, the path to a treasure is full of unexpected twists and turns. The only way to reach the clover is to brave the briars. Stick with it; the fortune is worth the ordeal.

Patience, Grasshopper.

MOST PEOPLE ENJOY STORIES WITH A HAPPY ENDING.

THIS ISN'T ONE OF THOSE BOOKS.

ADRIFT

Dusk fell hard on the massive trainyard, triggering thirty-seven
banks of LED lights designed to simulate daylight for numerous
workers scurrying about. Nocturnal critters hastened for the
shadows created by the low angles of the light banks. A lone
security officer donned his earphones—a defense against the
deafening rumble of four Dash 9 locomotive engines—and
began his final walkthrough of the westbound train. Satisfied
with the soundness of the couplings, and the lack of any
freeloaders on the cars, he radioed an "all clear" to the
conductor before starting his long walk back to the warmth of
his office.

Thick black diesel exhaust rose from the engines, one-
hundred and fifty cars clattered and began pulling out slack. The

sharp squeal of metal-wheel on metal-track pierced the air. Stacks of boxes filled with car parts and blenders, computers and neckties, knick-knacks and doo-dads, all began to gather speed for the monotonous journey west.

A shadow slid through a craggy hole in the perimeter chain link fence and dashed across the unused tracks. When he reached one of the slow-rolling high-top container cars, the shadow turned abreast, matching his speed with the lumbering giant. As its metal-rung ladder passed, he leaned forward and flailed out in an attempt to gain a hand-hold. His fingers missed the mark. His awkward forward lean, coupled with an alcohol buzz, caused him to lose balance. He fell face-first onto the loose gravel.

Get up, dammit.

The shadow scrambled to his feet and raced to match the speed of the next car in line. He reached for its ladder, this time meeting with success. He hoisted himself aboard the car, slung his heavy backpack onto the platform, and collapsed from exhaustion.

After regaining his breath, he sat up to watch the waning sunlight filter through the darkening trees. As they passed across the trestle bridge on the south-side of town, the light became scant; however, he could still make out the foamy white water of the river two-hundred feet below. Without thinking, he yelled at the top of his lungs into the chasm: "Hello!"

His own voice echoed back from the void, "Hello!"

The man laid back against his pack, taking in the vastness of the night sky. His emotions threatened to overwhelm him: *Your own voice is the only human interaction you've had in over a week.* He closed his eyes and succumbed to a combination of the alcohol, the melancholy, and the rocking of the rails. Before the next mile-marker passed, he'd collapsed into a deep slumber.

The alarm clock shrieked at four-fifteen AM. Janet hit the snooze button, thought better of it, and climbed out of bed. Despite the fact her husband would be leaving for a week away at work, she felt no desire to wake him. The irritation of their argument the night before persisted. She splashed water on her face, pulled her long brown hair into a ponytail, and slipped into her custom-made jumpsuit. Even in the faint light she could make out the embroidered sponsor patches sewn strategically onto the hot pink material. An involuntary yawn caught her off-guard. *Never mind the time, Jan, it's all about being a pro.*

She crept out of the room, pausing only to scratch the ears of her watchful Chihuahua. The rich smell of coffee wafted down the hall, courtesy of her automatic percolator. She pulled her pre-packed lunch out of the refrigerator, poured the coffee into her Thermos, stepped into the garage, and flipped on the light. She smiled at her brand new, hot pink, custom bass fishing boat. *That's what it's all about.*

Still grinning, she hit the switch for the automatic garage door opener and watched as it rolled up, gradually revealing a hot pink Dodge Ram pickup parked in the driveway. The boat was a necessity in her chosen profession, but the custom truck had been a gift to herself. Her husband hated it, which made it glow all the brighter in the moonlight. She unlocked it, threw her lunch and Thermos on the passenger seat, and backed it into the open garage to hitch up. Within ten minutes of waking, she made the right onto Baldwin Street and headed for the lake.

Her thoughts turned to her husband. *He's a good man.* She knew that from the bottom of her heart, yet she could feel the end of their marriage nearing. He wanted her to have a steady income, a stable schedule, and shared goals. *Shared goals meaning a baby.* The darkness of her mood matched the inky

4

night outside. *There's plenty of time for that later. I'm only twenty-five. I want what I want for now.*

She glanced in her rearview mirror at the behemoth attached to the hitch of her truck. An involuntary smile came to her. *I've only got one shot at my dreams.* She took a deep breath, assuring herself in the darkness. *And I'm going to take it. He can have his family—eventually.* She looked at the diamond ring on her left hand. *Even if it's with someone else.*

Her headlights revealed a large, brown sign on the left side of the two-lane road—Lake Thomas, two miles.

Come on, Jan. Concentrate on practicing for the Shimano Open. Everyone in the professional fishing universe will be there, and you can use more sponsors. Her brow furrowed. *Despite the fact he thinks I'm wasting my time out here.* She made a left and started down the boat ramp, her jaw tightened. *After all, it's my life.*

The floating of the boat went off without a glitch. Her practiced hands knew what to do, though her eyes still couldn't see the tasks before them. Her first cast landed among the reeds before the sun peeked over the low hills. All negative thoughts faded to silence.

The warm sun on his face woke the train-hopper. The voices inside his head started before his eyes even opened. He blinked furiously to clear the sleep, licking his dry lips as an afterthought. He groped around in his backpack and found a beer in an external pocket. Still cool, the first drops of the amber brew wet his whistle, bringing his throbbing head somewhat to heel. The remaining twenty-four ounces served as a makeshift breakfast. He pushed himself onto his elbows in an attempt to identify where the hell he was. The tracks ran in a long, straight line, carved out of a thick forest. *I wonder how far we've traveled.* He attempted some quick math in his head. *If a train leaves the station due west at sixty miles an hour—* He paused, his face scrunching into a frown. *And my life travels due east at a crawl...*

Fighting off tears, he scrambled to his knees and draped his arm over the safety rail. *Ah, Joe, what are you doing?* A thousand answers hit him at once, none of them soothing his funk. *Physically, you're searching for home.* He dropped his forehead against the cool metal and muttered to himself. The sound of his own voice caught him by surprise. "Mentally, you're searching for meaning."

You're running from your own pain, buddy. The thought sent him searching through his backpack, where he found a half-full bottle of cheap whiskey. *And the pain of everyone you've ever met.* He downed the contents in one long slug. The effects were immediate; his fingers numbed and his eyes grew heavy. Only the bottom of a bottle silenced the incessant chatter between his ears, yet it had no effect on his aching heart.

"God, I'm so lonely."

The statement surprised him, but it was the echoing voices of agreement that nearly overwhelmed his reality. *You have us to keep you company.* His jaw clenched. "You talk all the time, but you never say anything." *Now I'm talking back to myself.* He sat up in panic, climbed to the rail, searching through the shadows of the trees for any landmark. A faint blue hue shone through the gloom. *The sky?* A coolness in the air told him otherwise. *Water.* Within seconds, the rocky shoreline of a massive lake came into view.

Jan used the foot pedal of her trolling motor to ease her nearer to shore. She cast among the watercress, jigging her spoon lure through the loose leaves in search of hidden bass. To her dismay, not a single lunker took the bait. She reeled in, the line growing thicker on her spool, much like the apprehension in her chest. *I can't make a living if the damned fish don't cooperate.* She shook her head, the anxiety narrowing her throat.

What if he's right? What if I don't belong out here?

Her dad's face formed in her mind. Jan stood and turned in a full counterclockwise circle. "One to the left." She spun another circle in the opposite direction. "One to the right." Lovingly, she looked up at the sky. "Put your worries to bed for the night." She smiled. "Thanks, Dad."

Jan placed her pole on the rack and removed one rigged with a spook lure. She cast it off the opposite side and reeled in with jerks and pauses. Not even a nibble. Another cast produced a similar result. She switched poles to no avail. Six poles and lure combinations later, even her father's lucky charm had worn thin.

Jan reeled in; her mind fraught with fear. *Do I belong out here?* She forced herself to sit up straight, her line slack in the water. "He isn't right." She nodded to confirm her own words. *He talks all the time and never says anything worth a damn.* "I do belong out here."

The false bravado didn't work, her doubts rushed back, nearly overwhelming her. *I couldn't catch a cold.*

Her eyes darted to the rack of unlucky rods. "Keep fishing," she mumbled to herself.

Her mind swirled, and her doubts spoke with authority. *Physically, you're trying to catch fish, but you're actually fishing for answers.*

Ah, Jan, what are you doing? Her shoulders went slack. *My life is a sham.* She looked over the side of the boat at her own reflection. "Oh, God, I'm so lonely."

The mournful whistle of a passing train matched her tears.

The train-hopper caught a glimpse of a hot pink boat as the long caravan of boxcars passed out of the trees. He spied a lone figure sitting on the bow, rod parallel with the still lake water, a wet line disappearing below the surface.

Janet dried her eyes on her sleeve and glanced at the train plodding along the shoreline. She spotted a solitary rider perched on a boxcar, taking in the passing landscape as he placidly rode the rails to Wherever, USA.

"Damn, now that's how to be happy," they muttered in unison.

LINGER

Aqua Velva—the Classic Ice Blue stuff, not the skunky Musk crap they started selling in the '70's—was the last thing he remembered before losing consciousness. The edges closed in; shadows winning out over the vibrant colors of the sun-splashed park, yet the sharp, sweet tang of Aqua Velva pierced the falling veil. His eyes burned from the stench.

Of all the luck, I'm gonna smell like a barbershop when they bury me.

The kid looked up at the face of the punk standing above him, fist poised to deliver yet another blow. Through the cloying stink of the cheap aftershave and the stinging in his eyes, he caught a glimpse of the deep cut he'd made on the bully's face.

Blood oozed from a gash running diagonally from the corner of the thug's left eye to the center of his upper lip.

At least someone will have something to remember me by was his last thought as he succumbed to the darkness.

Two men worked feverously to revive their patient. The Denton FD paramedic rocked on his knees as he counted aloud the chest compressions performed on the good-as-dead kid's naked chest.

"One, and two, and three, and four, and five…

…A breath in time to keep him alive."

On the second syllable of the word *alive*, the ambulance attendant leaned forward, pinched the patient's nose, locked lips, and blew a rescue breath down his windpipe. The kid's chest rose, then fell slowly. As it reached level, the paramedic resumed his compressions.

The ambulance screeched to a stop at the emergency room entrance. The driver hurtled from his seat and yanked open the rear-double doors. Three men looked at each other and nodded in acknowledgment.

The nod set a gracious ballet into motion.

When the paramedic's sing-song cadence reached the correct moment, the ambulance attendant issued a rescue breath.

At the same time, the driver flipped the latch holding the gurney in place and jerked on the rail to start the bed rolling. The paramedic shuffled sideways, never breaking the rhythm of his compressions. The ambulance attendant grabbed the bed's interior rail and pushed forward. The driver eased the front wheels down and they touched the ground at the same time as the feet of the attendant. The back wheels of the gurney extended, touched the asphalt driveway, and rolled smoothly toward the emergency room. The paramedic never missed a stroke.

To the three professional lifesavers it was routine. To the unpracticed eye, the choreography was nothing short of exquisite.

Upon arrival at Bed Two of the emergency room, the ER team rushed into action. An EKG was set up. An oxygen mask was readied. A female nurse moved next to the paramedic. When the cadence reached the rescue breath stage, he stepped aside. When the compressions started afresh, she took over, pushing with the elegant strokes of a highly trained professional.

If Death wanted the kid, he'd have to fight for him.

Bret Hamlin, MD, the doctor on-duty, questioned the paramedic about the patient and confirmed the information from the firemen at the scene.

"The call came in of an unconscious male injured in the park," the paramedic said. "Unresponsive, but breathing when we arrived. Shortly thereafter, breathing ceased and he went into full arrest. We started CPR immediately."

"Do we know his name?"

"No. After we left, a police officer tracked down a neighbor who knew him. He went to the parent's house to inform them."

The doctor frowned and scrawled a few notes on the chart. He clicked his pen and put it in the pocket of his white smock. "Stop on the mark," his firm voice growled.

The nurse reached the end of her cadence and the ambulance attendant gave his final rescue breath. The CPR team took a step back. Everyone's eyes turned to the heart monitor. The ambulance attendant's gaze never left the kid's chest.

The man nearly fainted when his wife unraveled the situation over the phone. "I'll meet you at the hospital," was all he could choke out. He bolted from his corner office, through the maze of desks past the turned heads of his employees, and down three flights of stairs onto Central Ave. Not bothering to wait for his personal driver, he ran the six blocks to the hospital, custom silk necktie flapping in the breeze, arriving just as a police cruiser came to a stop in the emergency room red zone. The passenger door of the black and white flew open and the kid's distraught parents were reunited.

Mr. and Mrs. Wadsworth H. Honeycutt II sprinted frantically toward their dying son.

The veteran cop opened his trunk and took out his report-writing box. When ready, he strolled past the ambulance, closing the back doors out of professional courtesy. He stopped before entering the emergency room and frowned. From all the information he'd gathered at the scene, this was going to be a very sad case.

When the EKG showed a flat line, Doctor Hamlin picked up a pair of electrical paddles and stepped next to the bed.

"Clear!"

He zapped the patient; whose body rose involuntarily from the bed.

The team waited for an instant, the doctor pointed at the patient, and the chest compressions began anew—this time with a different nurse counting aloud. Ten cycles later the doctor called for another break. He stepped forward, called "Clear," and applied another shock.

Doctor Hamlin stepped back and said a silent prayer. *This can't go on forever.* He smiled as a faint, yet hopeful blip rose from the flat line.

Cloris Honeycutt sat stock-still in her chair—eyes closed, hands in a prayerful pose. Her husband sat next to her, mumbling a plea as his fingers absentmindedly picked lint from his expensive suit. Both looked up when the waiting room door opened.

Mr. Honeycutt's eyes widened when he recognized his golfing partner from the Seven Oaks Country Club. "Bret?"

The doctor offered a wan smile. "He's going to be okay, Worthy."

Mrs. Honeycutt erupted into tears.

In the corner of the room, the grizzled cop put down his report box, turned his head to hide his face, and wiped a tear off his cheek. He was a sucker for a happy ending.

That was twenty-two years ago…

The kid recovered—somewhat—from the beating. Emphasis on the somewhat. He was twelve years old at the time, recently completing the seventh grade. At an even five-feet tall, he was a normal-sized kid for his age.

As for the *somewhat*? Unfortunately, he never grew another inch.

The doctors blamed it on everything but the trauma; however, there were no other logical explanations. Both of his grandfathers topped out at over six feet and his dad had been even taller. Worthy Honeycutt certainly had his personal issues, God rest his soul; however, height wasn't one of them. He was six-three when he lost all his money in the Housing Bubble Burst of 2008. Even after he blew the top of his head off in the locker room of the country club, he was still six-one when they buried him.

The kid, real name Wadsworth Hayden Honeycutt III, fit as much fight into his stunted, wiry frame as he had grit into his thirty-four years on earth. His father's death left his mother in a financial bind, so the kid joined the military—US Air Force to be specific. After a successful stint as a jet engine mechanic, he moved back home to live with his mother, now the newly married Mrs. Bret Hamlin, MD.

Luckily, Doc Hamlin had a soft spot for his step-son. He graciously offered to adopt him, which was graciously declined. He graciously offered to send the kid through medical school, also graciously declined. In the end, Doc Hamlin added the kid's name to his will—as sole heir—and let him find his own path. The final offer was graciously accepted.

The training he'd received in the service helped the kid land a gig as an airline mechanic at the local international airport. He bought a small condo in the direct flight path of the planes he worked on, normally a deal breaker; however, the roar of the big engines rocked the kid to sleep like a lullaby.

Things were going along just peachy until Dr. Hamlin fell asleep behind the wheel of his Rolls Royce Phantom on the way home from Couple's Twilight Night at Seven Oaks Country Club. Mr. and Mrs. Bret Hamlin, MD, abruptly met their Maker in a muddy ditch a quarter mile from the off-ramp to their gated community.

The kid chalked it up to The Maker having something against his fathers, or members of the country club crowd.

Needless to say, after the life insurance policies were settled, the eight-bedroom mansion was sold, and Doc Hamlin's practice was purchased by his partners, Wadsworth Hayden Honeycutt III, now known affectionately as Waddy, turned into the richest man in seven counties.

As it has always been said, money cannot buy happiness; however, it did finance one of the kid's short-term fantasies— the richest man in seven counties bought himself a customized long-haul big-rig and ten lessons at the Debbie Dootson Driving School.

THE NOBODY

Vince Dolan was a nobody who desperately wanted to be a somebody, except—nobody cared.

He tried sports—nobody would let him play.

He tried various forms of the arts—nobody paid attention.

He went to culinary school—nobody liked his cooking.

Determined to become a somebody, Vince craved anybody's help; so, one night he met up with a group of nobodies with a *somebody* dream.

Vince joined a gang.

Not just anybody's gang, *everybody's* gang—the Mafia.

The problem is this: When somebody joins everybody's gang, they automatically start at the bottom of the ladder—as a nobody.

This didn't suit Vince. Being a nobody in everybody's gang was even more depressing than being a regular nobody-nobody.

It's not that the job they gave him was bad, he simply wanted more. He didn't know you had to work your way up to the whole extortion and murder end of the business. They ordered Vince to tend bar at the Missile Tow. Note: I did not say the Missile Tow Bar. Vince worked as a bartender in an actual tow yard.

This whole mess requires further explanation, so here's the scoop...

Al Falcone was a made-man from the Jersey side of the river. He got in a bloody scuffle with a member of the Philly syndicate, so the Bayonne Mob figured their guy needed a "vacation" until tempers cooled. As a result, they sent Al west and gave him a small towing company as a front for their money laundering activity.

Bayonne cooked Al's books, Al stayed out of Bayonne's hair.

Ba-da-bing, ba-da-boom.

Bayonne sent Al a stipend for two reasons—to live on and to keep his mouth shut. Yet, Al wasn't satisfied with the amount of money they sent, so he made use of the resources at hand and started an actual tow company.

Al made cash and Bayonne knew nothing about it.

Ba-da-bing, ba-da-boom.

Turns out Al was a dab-hand at business. He started with an old-fashioned hook and chain truck which he paid his nephew minimum wage to drive. The truck ran non-stop, making Al rich and his nephew complain.

Al fired his nephew and hired two locals to run the truck 24/7.

This made Al richer and his sister furious.

So, in the name of familial harmony, Al bought a flatbed and re-hired his nephew. That's when the real money started rolling in.

Another flatbed showed up, as did another pair of local drivers. A big-rig tow truck cost Al big bucks, but the big profits proved worthy. The tow business boomed and Al raked in the profits, half a country away from the prying eyes of the Jersey Familia.

But that's only part of the story. The good part is *the sign*.

Hanging above the entrance to the tow yard office was a hand-painted sign; red letters on a white background, framed by green boughs of mistletoe that read:

Missile Tow

If you don't like our service,

KISS OFF!

What started as a good-natured joke eventually caught the eye of a meddling do-gooder who fired off a hostile complaint letter-to-the-editor in the local paper. Of course, the effect was the exact opposite of which she'd hoped. The local story reached the desk of a special interest reporter from a national newspaper, whose story caught the eye of the producer of a national news report, whose television story caught the eye of...

You get the picture. The Missile Tow sign became a "must-see" attraction for tourists.

The do-gooder got so disgusted at the outcome of her attempt to clean up her city, she moved to Mississippi and started her own campaign to "Save Our Nation."

The problem for Al was this; business became so good at Missile Tow they outgrew their storage lot. No room remained for the tow fleet, the impounded cars, and visitors coming to see the sign. Al remedied that by purchasing an abandoned Blockbuster video store next to the old fairgrounds. He fenced in the fairgrounds parking lot, paved it, and moved his entire tow yard operation inside. He gutted the Blockbuster and put a door in the back for legitimate tow business.

In the middle, he built offices for the illegitimate operations.

Not done, Al partitioned off the front third of the building and built a bar, including pool tables and foosball. In a stroke of genius, he hung the Missile Tow sign above the front entrance. One quick call to an "associate" in the local media and a favorable article ran in the next Sunday paper. Presto, Missile Tow became the hottest hangout in town.

An empire was born. For a while.

But, back to Vince, after all, this story is about him.

Ain't it just like a nobody to have somebody hijack their story?

Al's first hire for the new bar was Vince Dolan. Actually, he had no choice but to hire him. It seems that the Bayonne boys exiled Vince west for having, "loose morals and sticky fingers."

Only Vince could get run out of the mob for not measuring up to their conduct policy.

Having zero prior mixology experience, Vince learned on the fly. More than once he confused a Manhattan for a Cosmopolitan, and his standard answer to a customer who asked for Sex On The Beach was, "Sure."

But learn he did.

With the addition of a jukebox and a small dance floor, Missile Tow became a gold mine for Al and Vince became a local legend. Problem was, the crowd was rough and the tips light. Vince wanted out.

Rolling in dough, Al bought a four-story high-rise downtown, in which he housed his family and the Bayonne-approved rejects. Al converted the ground floor into a swank tavern, called Naso Rotto, which served mostly as a cover for

Al's illicit gambling operation. The gang's headquarters also moved to the more comfortable digs, leaving Vince on his own most nights.

Vince asked Al a hundred different times to move from the Missile to the Naso, but Al wanted nothing of it. Vince was too valuable—the Missile patrons loved him.

Ain't it just like a nobody to screw themselves over by becoming a somebody?

After dislocating his pinky finger breaking up a violent scrap between a Missile Tow patron who'd had way too much to drink, and an actual customer livid because their Mazda had been towed—Vince reached the breaking point. The next time Al stopped by the Missile; Vince started in before Al even had a chance to order a drink.

"Hey, boss, ya gotta minute?"

Al didn't even give him the respect of looking his way. "You ain't moving."

"But, Al…"

"I told ya a thousand times, you're a rock star here."

Vince shook his head. "But, I'm miserable."

"So be miserable. Why should I give a—"

Vince played his hole card. "You know, I was wondering, do the Bayonne boys know how much dough you're making here? I'm sure they'd want their vig."

Al's fists clenched and his eyes narrowed. "Why, you ungrateful son-of-a-whore."

Vince flinched.

"Tell them," Al spat as he stood. "Tell them. And by the time they get here to check my books, your left nut will be in Tijuana and your right nut will be in Bangor, Maine." He towered over the barman who cowered in fear. "They'll find your body floating in the Gulf of Mexico with what's left of that little pecker of yours stuffed down your throat."

Al reached out and squeezed the lobes of Vince's ears.

"If you ever threaten me again, worm, I'll kill everyone in your family who ain't also related to me. Capisce?'

Vince blinked his eyes. He couldn't nod, Al had ahold of his ears.

Al turned him loose, slapped him full-force across the cheek, and left in a huff.

Vince's hole card turned out to be a miserable deuce.

The very next morning, Al's nephew towed the mayor's mother's Datsun. The mayor called Al for a favor. Still angry from the night before, Al didn't pay attention to the number on his caller ID. He answered the request with a string of Italian expletives that would have made Vito Genovese blush.

Within the hour, trucks from the City Streets Department descended on the area around Missile Tow. All roads in a two-block radius were closed for long-term maintenance, not to be reopened for a period of three-hundred and sixty-six days.

The Missile was dead-center of the blockages. Within a week, Missile Tow, both yard and bar, were wastelands.

Al never forgave Vince, believing him to be the one who broke the mojo of the entire Missile empire. He vowed to keep the bar open no matter how much it cost him. He also vowed Vince would tend bar every night under threat of death, even if the only customers were cockroaches. He changed the name to the Rendezvous and vowed to never step foot inside again.

"Call Bayonne now," Al sneered as he tossed Vince the last set of keys. "Maybe they'll find the place before you die of boredom."

No customers. No tips. No life.

Vince was screwed—like nobody's business.

29

Chasing Rats

Special Agent Doug Rawls slammed down the receiver of his phone so hard it cracked in half. Six agents from the FBI's Interstate Crimes Task Force looked up in unison.

"How do these bastards keep slipping through our fingers?" he screamed to the room.

"They've got 47,000 miles of Interstate freeways to hide on, Sir," someone answered.

Another agent cleared his throat and pointed to a large map of the United States. Push pins and red arrows covered the Midwest. "We've got them narrowed down to three states, Boss. We're tightening the noose."

Rawls turned to the plate glass window and gazed out at downtown Albuquerque. "They're really starting to piss me off."

"Me too," replied the agent closest to him. "Preying on struggling wage-earners. I miss working white collar crimes. Faceless victims are easier on the conscience."

"One of my victims couldn't pay the highway bandit's road tax last month," Agent Wanda Tremain said. "They beat him so bad he couldn't drive for a week. They stranded him fifteen-hundred miles from home unable to move—couldn't make his truck payment, so the bank repo'ed his big rig."

Rawls turned away from his own reflection in the glass and faced the room. "I just got off the phone with his widow."

Wanda Tremain's eyebrows shot up. "His widow?"

"She found him hanging from the rafters of their garage this morning."

Agent Tremain's eyes shut and her chin dropped.

"I want them caught," Rawls growled. "Whatever it takes. I know how much effort everyone's put into this, but we need to double it. We can add murder to the racketeering charges. That should be enough to get us some help. I'll get on the phone to Washington. You all get back to work."

Rawls paused at Wanda Tremain's desk and swallowed hard. "Take the rest of the day off, Wan," he said. "I know the news hit you hard."

Five other sets of ears strained for her response, struggling to hear over the incessant hum of the air conditioner and the crackling radio traffic on the police scanner.

Wanda looked up, eyes red-rimmed and mascara slightly smudged. Her reply was both audible and precise "I won't take another second off until these fuckers hang by the balls."

Rawls gave an emphatic nod. He straightened up; shoulders back, jaw stern. He peered at the others in the room, none of whom bothered pretending not to be listening. The deal was sealed. A professional understanding passed between them; an unspoken bond experienced only by those who've shared a singular, mutual goal. It might as well have been chiseled in stone. Not a single agent on the task force would rest until they completed the job. "You heard her, let's trap these rats."

Doug Rawls stomped to the only empty desk in the room, unclipped the receiver from its curly-cue cord, and replaced the one he broke on his own desk. With a steely determination, and a prideful sense of esprit de corps, he dialed FBI National Headquarters.

THE LETTER

The man sat on the exterior steps of the Amarillo Amtrak station
staring at a dog-eared envelope, its edges smudged from
constant handling. Every few seconds his head shook
involuntarily, yet his eyes remained fixed in marvel at the name
in the upper-left corner. Finally, he opened it and removed a
frayed letter, making sure the small, passport-sized photograph
and several newspaper clippings remained inside. Reaching into
the pocket of his dingy, black leather jacket, he removed his
Marlboro Reds, flipped a cigarette end-over-end, and caught it
deftly in his mouth. He lit it and took a long drag; the haze of
the smoke momentarily obscuring the letter, providing him a
brief respite from the mind-boggling words on the page. He
waved his hand to clear the air, bringing the first handwritten
line into sharp relief:

By the time you read this, I'll be dead. Unfortunately, that's where our story begins…

He dropped the envelope onto the step and scratched at the rough stubble of his beard, its wiry texture hiding the sharp edges of his hard-boned jaw. The fall jarred the photograph loose and it fluttered unseen onto the concrete near his feet.

He ran his fingers through his indigo hair. "I've seen some weird shit in my fucked-up life," he muttered to himself, "but this beats it all."

He closed his eyes so tight random shapes danced in the boundless void of the self-imposed darkness. Abruptly, he opened them, snatching up the envelope as he'd done countless times before. Somehow, just somehow, he hoped the names would change.

To: Joey Ianola, August, 2014.

"That's me alright." He rubbed his temples to relieve some stress. *Damned near five years ago.*

His eyes meandered to the overwhelmingly familiar name in the corner.

From: Joey Ianola, August, 2019.

The air burst from his lungs in a familiar panic. *It can't be true.* He glanced at the date on the letter then back to the names—all equally unbelievable.

The sudden sound of approaching footsteps startled him. He sat up, folded the letter, and slid it out of sight.

A bum carrying a dirty backpack stopped at a nearby trashcan and began digging for scraps in anticipation of an afternoon meal. Noticing the forlorn man on the stairs for the first time, the bum grumbled, "You look like someone who needs to talk."

Joey glanced sideways at him, taking in the kind eyes and prominent smile-lines around the drifter's mouth. A sudden calm settled on him. When he spoke, his voice revealed the depths of his gloom. "Brother, you don't have enough time."

The bum flopped onto the steps. From his pack's main compartment, he withdrew an unopened pint of Jack Daniels. He extended the bottle toward his newfound companion. "I've got nothing but time. Give me a try."

Joey nodded in thanks and didn't hesitate, ripping off the seal and drawing a long slug of the harsh liquid.

The bum pointed to the wayward photo. The face of a clean-shaven man wore a half-smile, yet his eyes carried a deep sadness. "Your brother?"

Shocked someone else had seen the picture, the ramifications threatened to overwhelm Joey. Another glance at the bum's soulful eyes removed all anxiety. Without a word, he handed him the letter.

The bum's finger passed over the writing and his lips formed the words as he read in silence. When he finished, he held up the photo to contrast it with Joey's face.

"Prank?" He shook his head. "Can't be, he's got the same mole as you."

A wry smile crossed Joey's lips. "If it's a prank, I've never seen its rival."

The bum chuckled. "Joey Ianola. That name sounds familiar."

Joey handed him the envelope.

The bum removed the newspaper clippings. The first was a headline story from the New York Times: LOCAL BOY STRUCK BY LIGHTNING—CAN READ FUTURE. The second was from the Wall Street Journal: YOUTH TURNS TRAGEDY INTO WINDFALL. Another was from the back page of the New York

Post: LOCAL NUT CLAIMING MAGICAL POWERS. The final item was a story from the National Enquirer containing a hand-drawn caricature depicting Joey's teenaged face with lecherous eyes, a lascivious sneer, and colossal ears. The headline dubbed him: FUTURE BOY.

The bum's face softened. "Yeah, now I remember."

"Everything you remember is exactly what I want to forget."

"Fame sucks, huh?"

Joey grimaced. "Yes, it does."

The bum re-read the letter, then glanced at the envelope. "A harsh life in the public eye is one thing…" He whistled through his teeth. "But this—this is something else entirely." He held up the clippings in one hand. "These say you can read the future." He held up the letter in the other. "But this was actually *from* five years in the future. That, my friend, is a scoop!"

"I received it in August, 2014, almost five years ago, so the stuff from the papers is already old news," Joey sighed. "But, supposedly—yes, it's a letter written five years in the future. Even in the four years and ten months I've had it, I still can't wrap my head around what it says." Joey looked up, his moist eyes betraying his hard exterior. "And now I'm up against a deadline of death."

"The bewilderment is understandable. Death, in and of itself, is a daunting mystery. But, to have an implied knowledge of the end date on your own headstone; well, that's an absolute terror." The bum pulled on his ear, a thousand miles away in thought. "And he—no, you—knew you'd never believe it. Hence, the photograph."

"I guess I got more cunning as I aged."

"Why not make this public? It could only help, you know—credibility-wise."

"Help? Society doesn't want help. They only want *people* and *things* they can use to benefit themselves."

The bum stared at Joey, looking as if, for all the world, nothing surprised him. "So now you spend your time drunk at train stations? Seems like a waste of a useful talent."

"Don't get me wrong, I've used my talents—as they are—but for seemingly all the wrong reasons. I've made tons of cash, lived high-on-the-hog, and hobnobbed with some hard-core VIPs." He locked eyes with the drifter. "I've done," he grinned, "some seriously fun shit."

"That's how you've used…?"

"Well, I did *some* good for society, but the media had its way with me to the point where I wanted nothing else to do with them. So now, here I am, facing my own mortality. I'm done, brother. I deserve some—*time off.*"

"Ha, time off, good one," the bum said. "There's only one problem with your theory."

"Theory? What do you mean? I don't have a theory. If, like the letter says, I wrote—" Joey paused to gather his thoughts, "I also said I'd be dead by August, 2019. That's only a little over a month away."

"There are infinite ways it might not happen."

Joey's jaw clenched. "So, now *you're* the one with a theory?"

"You're going to have to trust me on this, but there's no way you could've predicted your own death five years ago and fired off a warning letter. It's just not that simple to do."

"Yeah, that's the one loophole I found in the entire gig. Still, now it's so close, it's scaring the hell out of me."

"Seems to me the logical thing is to proceed forward at all costs. Stay in the light."

"What do you mean?"

"Live as if you'll live forever—it just might come true."

"At this point in my miserable existence," Joey shrugged, "how can I justify the effort?"

"Because all other options lead to death." The drifter took a deep breath and exhaled slowly. "Take it from me—death ain't all it's cracked up to be."

Joey stared at the man in wonder, his mouth asking questions that found no voice.

The bum squinted at the letter, reading a specific passage aloud. "*Heed what the Buddha tells you, and for crissakes, Joey—save the boy.* What's that mean?"

"I have zero clue."

"No matter. It's solid advice." The bum stood. "I've got a bus to catch. You keep the bottle; it looks like you'll need it."

"Gee, thanks. I don't know how to…"

The bum shouldered his pack. "Joey, there's wisdom in that letter, prank or not. I'd believe everything in there if I were you. And another thing…" He turned to leave. "If you do meet the actual Buddha, I'd take his word as gospel."

With that, the bum disappeared into the building.

Joey gathered his things to leave, stealing one last glance at the envelope with its matching names in both the "to" and "from" positions. He swallowed hard at the implications and put the clippings and the photo back inside. Something in the ether of his mind spoke to him. He opened the tri-folded page for what seemed like the millionth time and re-read the closing line.

Good luck, Joey. We're both going to need it—Me.

Bolstered somewhat by the knowledge the letter's date assured him of at least one more month to live, Joey donned his grimy leather jacket and shuffled off to find a nearby bar.

WADDY

Wadsworth Hayden Honeycutt III was not your typical long-haul trucker. Waddy's diminutive stature set him apart from the burly he-men who normally drove cross country. This had always been a problem, although not so much anymore. The fact is, he drove for pleasure, not for profit. His stepfather's untimely demise provided him said luxury. While others scrambled to stretch their driving hours and fudged their logbooks, Waddy worked when he wanted.

But, work he did.

He was his own boss and his only boss. He took orders from no one and suffered no fools. His adherence to the Code of the Road was as strict, if not more so, than a driver working on the narrowest margin. His go-to phrase? *If you're gonna do it, do it right.*

Waddy carried himself with a dignity and pride uncommon in the trucking field.

All this said: In the solitary, isolated world of the long-haul trucker, no one bothered to notice any of the above.

Waddy's only connection to the others making a living on the road was an occasional squawk on the CB about a lurking Highway Patrolman or yielding to faster trucks on steep inclines. Aside from those interactions, he lived by the Code: "Stay out of my way, I have bills to pay." Waddy's standing in the trucker brotherhood remained on solid ground.

Except with the Turk Mullins Gang.

Turk Mullins, real name Gerald, was a high-school dropout from Tuscaloosa, Alabama. What Turk lacked in scholarly aptitude, he made up for in sheer hostility. Twelve years prior, Turk made the mistake of dropping his wallet during the commission of a bank robbery in Terra Haute, Indiana. A truck driver on a short-hop haul from Muncie to Decatur found the wallet at the scene and provided the billfold, plus a description of the man who dropped it, to local police. That misfortune cost Turk ten years in the federal pen.

Upon his release, Turk hitchhiked from Terra Haute to Lincoln, Nebraska. Well, technically it could be considered hitchhiking. When the car's owner asked Turk to drive so he could get some shut-eye, Turk pulled off the highway and dumped his sleeping passenger, sans his wallet, in the parking lot of a White Castle in Davenport, Iowa. Therefore, the last three-hundred and fifty-three miles were, in actuality, a carjacking.

From there forward, Turk Mullins spent every waking hour pillaging truck drivers in a misguided attempt at retribution for the man who innocently found his wayward billfold at the scene of a holdup. Turk's criminal enterprise grew from one thug, himself, to three with the addition of his drinking buddies, the Charles brothers. Money rolled in from a series of package thefts, robberies, and outright extortions. With the addition of Phil Hokeman, Turk's old prison cellmate, the four-man team drifted from Lincoln to Albuquerque where they began preying upon truckers hauling goods from Texas to California along I-40. The truckers rarely fought back, seeing as how their loads were insured and their wages guaranteed. Therefore, the theft and robbery business were both semi-safe and lucrative from the get-go. The boys were soon rolling in the profits.

In a stroke of nefarious genius, Turk sent the Charles brothers on interstate road trips to commit random robberies as a means to throw off any cops trying to map out their operations. It was on one of those road trips the brothers met, and semi-befriended, a hard-ass goon from down Texas way by the name of Nate Hicks. A true mouth-breathing hooligan, Nate knew he was tougher than everyone in the room and he expected them to acknowledge that fact or run the risk of a hearty introduction to his gnarled fists. Nate's bulging muscles and scarred face cemented the fact that no one, not even Turk himself, wanted to tangle with the brute.

Upon Nate's uneasy acceptance into the fold, Phil got the brilliant idea of capitalizing on the newcomer's talents. He proposed they begin strong-arming truckers for what he deemed a "roadway tax." Phil figured the government charged a toll along main routes, so why shouldn't they? Once Phil pointed out the monetary upside, Turk readily agreed. They elected Nate, muscles bulging from his ears, as the gang's Tax Collector.

Some folks are just born with useful talents.

MELE MARCE

The only person who hated Al Falcone more than Vince Dolan was Knuckles Pecota. Thought to be the successor to the local capo position before Al was sent west, Knuckles had been relegated to a lowly enforcer position upon arrival of the new boss. Thinking he was a shoo-in for the windfall the capo position represented, Knuckles bought himself a new Lincoln. There's a reason why his nickname was Knuckles and not Brains. By the way, the only person who thought Knuckles was destined for capo was Knuckles himself. Everyone west of Bayonne knew Knuckles as a coward. For that matter, so did everyone in Bayonne.

So did his wife, which is why she busted his chops every waking hour.

"We need more money."

Knuckles tied his shoe. "I know, dear."

"Did you call Bayonne for a raise?"

Knuckles checked his tie in the mirror. "I didn't have time today."

"We need a bigger house."

Knuckles donned his hat. "Put a bunk bed in the boy's room, your mom can have the spare."

"You need to talk to Al. We ain't got a pot to piss in since you bought your stupid car."

Knuckles pecked her on the cheek. "We'll make do."

"Make do hell! You need a raise!"

Knuckles trundled down the steps and slid into the Lincoln. The sound of a revved engine drowned out the persistent harangue.

Knuckles found Lefty Salducci picking at his fingernails on the sidewalk in front of his house. Lefty flicked his cigarette butt onto the street and slid inside the car.

"Whassup, Knucks?"

"Hey, Lefty. How's it hanging?

"I'm glad you showed up, my old lady's on a rampage."

50

Never one to mix his family with business, Knuckles bit his lip.

Lefty noticed. "How's come you never talk about your wife, Knucks?"

"Work ain't the place."

"Fuck that, you're just scared she'll hear about it through the grapevine and box your ears." Lefty chuckled at his own joke. "Everybody please bow your heads and observe a moment of silence for Knuckles Pecota's testicles."

Knuckles considered himself a tough guy, muscle of the outfit, but Lefty was the gang's eraser: a steely-eyed hit man. Knuckle's bit his tongue. "She ain't so bad, Lefty. You just need to get to know her."

Lefty sneered. "Last time I seen her she had more paint on her face than a camouflaged tank."

Knuckles slammed on the brake, fully intending to break a bone or two. Lefty got the drop on him, slapping the bigger man across his face. Knuckles saw red, but froze in place when he felt the cold steel barrel of a revolver in his ribs.

"Calm down, Knucks. Just havin' a little fun."

The bean counter was the last stop for the gangster carpool. As the accountant, Specks Johansen had accumulated significant financial resources, as well as a huge house in a tony neighborhood near downtown. Specks had neither the size, nor the physical weapons to participate in the usual rough banter, so he rode in silence, speaking only when necessary.

That trait pissed Lefty off even more than Knuckles' cowardice. "A man who don't talk is hiding something," Lefty always said.

As if the mansion alone wasn't enough of a clue.

The last seven miles of the drive to the Naso were normally made in silence—not today. Already agitated from his confrontation with Knuckles, Lefty felt bold. "What is it about you, Specks, too good to talk to us?"

The smaller man stretched out his right index finger and pushed his glasses higher up the bridge of his nose. "I've got nothing good to say."

"Why's that? You're well taken care of—the boss's pet even. Why you got nothing good to say?"

The little man's upper lip trembled. "Don't get me started."

Lefty took out his five-shot revolver, twirling it on his finger like a movie star cowboy. "I say you start."

The dam burst on five years of silence. "It's always the same thing in this boring gang. You pick on the yellow baboon, he complains to Al about money, Al complains to me about you two, and I sit there and take it. It's all one big whine-fest and card games."

Lefty spun on his seat. "Don't you say nothing bad about the boss."

"He cheats at cards. Hides aces all over the place. Robs you two fools blind."

Lefty leveled the gun at the accountant's heart. "You can't say something like that. It just ain't right!"

The scowl on the accountant's face was more profane than any combination of words sworn in anger. "I can say any damned thing I want. I sign your checks."

Lefty's face screwed up in fury, which quickly abated when he realized Specks was one-hundred percent right. He lowered the gun and turned back toward the windshield.

A silly grin crept onto Lefty's face. It lasted until he parked the Lincoln at the Naso.

PISS STOP

Waddy Honeycutt needed to whizz. His fuel gauge read a
quarter tank, so he pulled into a desolate, but well-lit Pilot Super
Stop in Tijeras, New Mexico and slid his rig between a short-
haul three-axle and an ancient Peterbilt flat-bedding a backhoe.
Waddy wriggled his hundred and twenty-four-pound frame out
of his luxurious leather seat and shimmied down to the running
board using the faux-pearl handhold. He paused at the front
wheel well, took out his handkerchief, and polished a smudge
off his custom-painted Volvo VNL 760 semi. Something about
the size and splendor of his truck provided Waddy with a
serenity that nothing else in the world came close to matching—
except maybe the ten-gallon Stetson he'd treated himself to in
Dallas. The sheer girth of the brushed-felt beauty was majestic
enough, yet the rattlesnake band was the cherry-on-top.

Waddy sighed at the grandeur of the Volvo. He had no home and no one he held so dear as to even dream about returning to, so his rig sufficed as a permanent address. He strolled toward the Pilot in as good a mood as he had a right to expect.

When two dark-haired ruffians stepped into his path, Waddy knew his luck had changed.

"Headed to LA?" the taller goon asked.

Waddy glared up at the thug. "Who's asking?"

"I'll do the questioning around here, little fella. You just come in off of I-40?"

Waddy turned in an exaggerated three-hundred and sixty-degree arc, taking in the vast expanse of flat desert. "Do you see any other roads out here?"

The stockier of the two men scowled and took a step toward Waddy, who countered with two steps to the rear.

"Stop," the taller man barked. Waddy had no intention to listen.

The thicker man froze mid-stride. *The tall one's giving orders*, Waddy thought. He snuck a quick glance at the two men who had similar features and matching eyes. *Brothers*.

The taller man cracked his knuckles. "We run this area. The Forty is ours. You want to work it, you pay—us."

Waddy grimaced at their gall. "If there's one thing I can't stand, it's a bully." He pierced both men with a stare. "The only thing worse is two of 'em."

The thicker brother's eyes blazed. "Gonna be tough driving your fancy rig with broken thumbs."

Waddy had met a thousand men like these two in his life. Big and tough, sure that their size would intimidate smaller prey. The thing is, Waddy ate bullies for breakfast. He pushed his hat back on his head. "Fuck you."

The thicker man charged him. Used to fighting men of his own size, he miscalculated. Waddy slipped beneath his outstretched arms and jammed his jagged truck keys into the bigger man's gonads. He went down hard, writhing in pain.

His brother turned to make sure he wasn't hurt seriously. Bad mistake.

Waddy jumped inside his truck and had the engine revved before the thug could turn back around. The taller brother reached into his waistband, withdrew a handgun, and fired. In his haste, he completely missed the Volvo. Waddy dropped the engine into low gear and popped the clutch. The truck jumped forward.

The taller man fired again without looking, then scrambled to drag his brother from harm's way. In the melee, he tripped, landed on his brothers' torso, and rolled to a stop near the middle of the island. He fired again, hitting the Volvo's front bumper.

Enraged, Waddy gunned the engine and the rig's right-front tire rolled over the taller man's legs, pulverizing his bones.

His scream roused his brother. Taking in what happened, the thicker man jumped onto the passenger-side running board and began pulling at the door to get inside. Waddy jerked the wheel and the goon tumbled hard to the pavement. Waddy gunned the engine and hit the on-ramp at full speed.

Without thinking, the thicker brother jumped into a fire engine-red Mercedes, leaving his brother to thrash about in agony. He pushed the luxury car's accelerator to the floor and pulled abreast of the passenger-side of the Volvo within five miles. He rolled down his window and brandished a handgun, screaming at Waddy to pull over or die.

Waddy took in his surroundings and smiled as a large overhead sign came into view. It read, Highway 14 exit, ½ mile.

The goon's first shot skipped off the hatch of the overhead sleeping compartment, the resulting echo reverberated throughout the cab. That pissed Waddy off even further. The second shot broke the glass out of his sideview mirror. The Mercedes sped up until it reached a half-a-car-length in front of the truck. The goon waved his gun wildly and screamed at Waddy to pull over.

Waddy knew if he could see the man's eyes, the man's eyes couldn't see what was coming. He floored it and jerked the wheel hard to the right. In his rage, the car's driver had no time to react as the truck hit him broadside. Waddy steered even harder to the right, pushing the Mercedes over the side and down the embankment of the Highway 14 underpass. It tumbled sideways, flipped twice, and slammed sidelong into a concrete abutment.

Waddy could barely make out a trail of smoke rising from the burning vehicle as he crested the rolling hills surrounding Albuquerque.

Chad Charles was already writhing in the back of the ambulance when the first police officer arrived on scene. The fresh-faced

New Mexico State Trooper stuck his head in the door. "What the hell happened here?"

"That guy just went crazy," Chad screamed through the pain. "He started beating my brother and me up for no reason. Then the bastard ran me down."

A black Chevy Impala with dark-tinted windows rolled up. An impeccably dressed man hopped out of the car and sauntered up to the ambulance. He flashed his badge to the State Trooper. "What's going on here?"

The Trooper's brow furrowed. "What's the FBI want with a highway dispute?"

"We're handling a string of interstate trucker embezzlement and strong-armed robberies, possibly even some murders to tag on."

Chad's upper lip twitched. "The idiot demanded our money, said there's a roadway tax. When we refused, he went crazy and started beating both of us up."

The Trooper's eyebrow cocked. "Why didn't you tell me this before?"

Chad's eyes dropped. "Because he's a little fella. Kinda embarrassing having him rob me."

The FBI agent took out his field notebook and opened it to a fresh page. "It looks like he might have just murdered someone, as well. Forced a car over the embankment near Highway Fourteen."

Chad's mouth dried and he choked on his words. "What kind of car?"

"A red Mercedes by the looks of what's left."

Not wanting to betray his own story, Chad Charles bit back bitter tears for his hot-headed brother. Despite himself, he began to whimper, which blossomed into a full-blown wail when the State Trooper spotted the butt of a large-caliber Ruger sticking out of the patient's waistband.

THE RELUCTANT HERO

The square-jawed Secret Service agent raised his left arm and spoke into the microphone hidden in his sleeve. "The Eagle's away." Dozens of police officers on motorcycles moved into position, shutting down intersections in anticipation of the fast-moving motorcade.

The President sat back on his luxurious leather seat and sighed, "What's next?"

Todd and Megan Williams tightened helmets on their children's heads and made sure the snaps were secured. "We need to hurry," Megan said. "The news said his meeting's over at noon."

"Let's go," Todd nodded.

Their daughter, Alexa, pushed down hard on her pedal and her bicycle lurched forward with a jump. At ten years old, she was sure she knew which way to go and that the others would follow.

Maddox glanced up at his father for assurance. Todd smiled at the red-faced towhead, and the youngster's confidence grew. He began to pedal, slowly at first, staying close enough to not lose sight.

Megan rode abreast of her daughter, who was eager to see the President in her hometown. They chatted about the car he drove, and which town he was scheduled next.

Todd rode ahead of his son, his impatience fueled by his slow-poke eight-year old and thoughts of a big project at work in danger of failing.

"Daddy!"

Todd turned around to see Maddox in tears. "What's the matter, son?"

"Slow down, I can't keep up."

Todd's ears reddened. "Pedal faster or we'll miss the motorcycles. You're not going to fall."

Todd hung back until Maddox was in motion, then started pedaling hard to catch up to his wife. *Dammit! I knew I should have skipped this. Now I'm going to miss the whole thing and lose the time I could've been working.*

Maddox cried all the way to Main Street.

When the train slowed to a crawl outside the local yard, a shadow jumped from one of the low-boy cars and sprinted into the bushes. Satisfied he wouldn't be seen; he climbed the perimeter fence and went in search of alcohol.

A pub is what I need. Beer and a pickled egg.

Following his instincts, he made a right on Third Street. *Third Streets always connect with Main. There's where the bars will be.*

When he reached the red, white and blue bunting and the five-deep crowd, he knew he'd screwed up. *What the hell's going on?*

He turned up the collar of his dusty, black leather jacket and pulled his watchman's cap low over his ears. *Too many people to find a bar. A liquor store'll have to do.*

Todd Williams found the motorcade route and the mass of people lining it, but he couldn't find Megan and Alexa. He got off his bike and led Maddox to an opening in the crowd.

"Daddy, where's Mommy?"

"I don't know, son. Keep your eyes open for her."

"Daddy, I can't see anything."

In his irritation, Todd tuned him out.

The shadow walked quickly down the sidewalk, tucked between the teeming crowd and the dingy downtown buildings. *What the hell are all these people doing here?*

One word echoed in his ears. "President."

He shook his head. *Just my luck, I get off the train in the middle of a circus.* He started to count his steps to drown out the chatter of a thousand voices filling his thoughts. *Find a six-pack and get the hell outta Dodge.*

Todd Williams heard the approaching sirens and knew what it signified. "Move closer, son. They're almost here."

"But, Daddy, I can't see anything."

The first pair of motorcycles passed in a blur and the crowd surged forward. Todd scoured the masses for Megan and Alexa to no avail. A second set of motorcycles whizzed by and Todd knew the limousines would be next. He craned his neck to watch.

"Daddy!" Maddox whined to himself. "I can't see."

The din of the crowd thickened. Clapping and chants of support made normal conversation impossible. Through it all, the shadow heard the voice of a child as if he were standing at his side.

I can't see.

He glanced up, just in time to see the young boy push hard on the pedal of his bike, driving it toward the street.

He's going into traffic.

His mind began a debate.

So what, it's not my problem.

 Come on, Joey. You can't let him die.

Why not? He's not my boy.

 Because, dammit, he's only a kid, Joey. You can't NOT do it!

Reason won out. The shadow darted through the crowd in the instant Maddox Williams rode in front of the President's limo. He grabbed the boy by the waist and yanked him toward the sidewalk. The limo hit the bicycle at over fifty miles-an-hour. The crushed bike flew over the crowd and smashed through the window of a street-side barbershop.

As per Federal policy, the Presidential limo continued on, but three Chevy Suburbans full of Secret Service agents screeched to a halt. Men in dark suits swarmed from the vehicles in search of answers.

Realizing what happened, Todd Williams ran to his son, wrapping his arms around him. Both began to weep.

The shadow rose quickly and scampered back into the throng. A burly man with a long, gray beard grabbed him by the arm, pulling him face-to-face. "Mister, you saved that boy's life!"

The first Secret Service agent reached Maddox Williams at the same time a member of the press saw the burly man detaining the squirming shadow.

"What's going on here?" the reporter asked.

"This fella saved that boy. It's almost like he knew it was gonna happen."

Special Agent Tom Timmons overheard the statement. He immediately radioed the lead Secret Service limo, which was caught on the scanner by local police—and the press.

Squirm as he may, the shadow was now a hero.

News of the Presidential limo striking a bicycle along a motorcade route instantly became prized news. Within seconds, thousands of photographs, and millions of bytes of footage were recorded by several opportunistic news teams and a phalanx of ravenous citizens armed with cell phones.

The voices in the shadow's head screamed louder than even the gathered mass could match.

When the Senior Correspondent from local Channel Four showed up, he recognized the face in an instant. "Hey, you're Joey Ianola!"

It wasn't until the national news trucks arrived that Joey fully realized his predicament. The chatter in his head reached a crescendo, but his own voice cut through the racket.

Run!

When the boom went up on a CNN truck and the reporter shouted to the cameraman, "Roll tape," Joey took the cue and disappeared into the frenetic horde. He didn't stop until he was back on a westbound freight car.

Screw the beer. He'd done the celebrity thing before, and it was far too noisy.

AH, NOT AGAIN

A full twenty-four hours had passed since the incident in Tijeres and Waddy's nerves were still jangled. After dumping his freight at a huge retail hub in east Albuquerque, he picked up a full load at the airport and resumed his journey west. He exited the highway using the Unser Boulevard off-ramp and eased his rig into a lazy truck stop in search of some fuel, rest and hot grub. He rumbled to a stop near the main pumps, slid out of the cab and locked his door. As Waddy's rotten luck would have it, he didn't make it to dinner.

A heavily-muscled, scar-faced goon appeared as if from nowhere, his booming voice rife with aggression. "And just where do you think you're going?"

71

Waddy glared up at the thug, taking in the Texas accent. "Who's asking?"

"The name's Nate Hicks. I'm the tax collector 'round these parts." He spat out his chaw near the driver's boot. "I hear tell we've got us a little fella who's refusing to pay his fair share. It's not good for business for me to allow such nonsense."

"Ah, hell, not again," Waddy muttered. He sneered at the giant towering over him and bowed his neck. "Ain't taxes collected in April?"

Nate's fists tightened at the snide comment.

"My name is Waddy."

"Woggy? What's your given name, Pollywog?"

Waddy's blood boiled, but he stood his ground. Tears filled his eyes at the restraint.

Nate offered a stupid half-smile. "Why, you ain't nothing but a mad crybaby."

Waddy noticed the scar running diagonally from the corner of the thug's left eye to the center of his upper lip. His eyes narrowed and recognition heightened his senses. "I don't want another incident like Tijeres, Nate."

"The easy solution is to give me your road tax, Woggy."

"I drive truck to stay away from bullies, Nate. I don't pay taxes to anyone, especially you. You're not the Governor."

"I see myself more as a President, Woggy. And I'm my own one-man army." Nate drew out a switchblade.

Unbowed, Waddy thrust out his chest. "I didn't pay before and I ain't paying now."

The muscles in the thug's neck tightened and a vein throbbed on his forehead.

Waddy used his words in an attempt to throw the goon off balance. "What's a Texas boy doing all the way over here in New Mexico?"

Nate shrugged his shoulders. "I've been working for a local racket run by a guy named Turk Mullins here in Albuquerque, scamming hokey taxes off of stiffs like you. The pay's good," Nate bragged. "Turk sees to it." When he finished, Nate took a half-step forward.

Waddy read the danger in the movement, squaring his own body in preparation for an attack. "Why are you telling me all this?"

"No harm in it," Nate said as the switchblade popped open. "Cuz, you know—yo ho, yo ho, dead men tell no tales." He lunged for Waddy who easily ducked beneath the

73

outstretched knife. Nate's torso bumped hard against Waddy's face.

It was the overwhelming stench of Aqua Velva that gave him away.

Wadsworth Hayden Honeycutt III snapped. Adrenaline surged into his veins, filling him with the strength of ten men the size of Nate Hicks. In a rage, he rammed his shoulder into the bully's leg, tripping him against the raised curb.

Nate bounced off the pump and fell sideways, landing hard against the concrete. The whole thing happened so fast he couldn't get his hands up to protect himself. His own knife stabbed him in the leg and his head snapped violently against the cold cement. Dazed, the bigger man sat up, wondering where the hell he was.

Without thinking, Waddy snatched the spigot off the pump and squeezed. A surge of premium, ninety-two octane gasoline shot out of the nozzle, covering Nate Hicks. Waddy aimed at the thug's mouth and guided the stream down his spluttering throat. Choking on the noxious fuel, Nate kicked and flailed in an attempt to stand, yet gained no foothold on the slippery liquid.

Waddy dropped the spigot and took a step back. His vision narrowed and his thoughts focused only on what lay before him—the bully whose vicious beating twenty-two years prior had destroyed his life. Nate struggled to reach him but slipped, landing on his back in the middle of the island. Waddy's rage consumed his judgment. He took out his lighter, slapped it open to spark a flame, and tossed it onto the puddled gasoline near the bully's legs. Nate screamed in recognition. His clothes caught fire first and he thrashed about wildly in an attempt to snuff out the flames.

It wasn't until the gasoline in Nate's stomach exploded that Waddy knew vengeance was his.

As people began streaming from the Pilot, the little man picked up his hat, straightened the rattlesnake band, and slid unnoticed into the shadows. He pissed behind a low-slung pucker-bush and climbed back into the Volvo. When his adrenaline ebbed and the realization of fear replaced the false bravado, he broke into a sweat and began shaking. He clambered into the sleeper-cab, pulled a blanket over his head, and wept uncontrollably.

After crying himself to sleep, he dreamt of vanilla ice cream.

THE ONE THAT GOT AWAY

The water on Lake Thomas was just right. The wind and temperature told Jan that the bass should be feeding, yet she couldn't coax a bite for trying. The sky above was clear, yet dark clouds formed in her heart.

Damn it, Janet. Face facts. You're not a professional and you never will be. Tears streamed down her face as she cast out for what could be the last time. She paused and wiped her cheek with her sleeve. Before her hand touched her reel, she began to shake. A quarter-mile from the dock, she collapsed into convulsive sobs.

When the outburst abated, Jan took stock. Her life centered around becoming a professional angler. Not her husband. Not her home. *Fishing.*

Yet, with all her experience and the best gear money could provide, she couldn't land a thing. The thought irked her. *You've had cold streaks before. What's this really about?*

"Him." Saying it aloud brought everything into the light.

"His job's the only thing he loves." She'd guessed at this before, but now it was obvious.

"He leaves Sunday night and doesn't come home until Friday." She was aware this would be the case when she married him. Federal employees served at the whim of Washington. They didn't care if families were split, they needed people on both coasts.

"Yet, he wants me to stay at home and give him a family." Her eyes burned. *It just isn't fair.* "A life lived that way isn't conducive to my happiness." The words felt selfish, yet the clouds around her heart dissipated when she spoke.

"I don't want to live where he works, especially since where he works shifts on a whim. I want to live here." She felt the sturdy boat beneath here and a gentle breeze off the water. "This is home."

She reeled in; her mind made up. She dialed the number without hesitation, her hands steady as the boat rocked gently in the breeze. His answer was rushed, as it often was, with no hint of greeting.

"Now's not a good time, Jan."

"It's never a good time for you."

"Make it brief, I'm in the middle of something."

"I want a divorce." The words released the tension in her soul.

The silence on the other end was total. She imagined his lips moving up and down in shock. His reply belied no such distress "Not now, Jan. Like I told you, I'm in the middle of something important."

The lack of compassion in his voice steeled her conviction. She glanced around at the gorgeous lake, its shores emerald green in the distance. She slipped off her ring and flung it into the deep-blue water. "I'm in the middle of something important, as well. And, unlike you, I love it because it's always here for me! I don't want the life you've mapped out for me; I want my own life. Good luck with whatever's so important. Maybe it'll tuck you into bed tonight!"

She tossed her phone into her tackle box and glanced up at the sky. *That's that.* She inhaled deeply, releasing it in a long, slow stream. The anxiety that had weighed on her for months followed the breath from her lungs and disappeared into the crisp mountain air.

Instinctively, Jan picked up her rod and cast her line without thinking. She jerked the line and started to reel. In a rush, the tip bent nearly parallel to the water.

Even the fish knew the time was right.

THE HITCHHIKER

The dark gathered quickly in the Midwest plains as the driver turned onto the four-lane highway, reached high-gear, and settled into his overstuffed-seat for a long stretch. Traffic thinned as the midnight hour loomed and he found himself alone with his thoughts. One simple question pushed out all other voices, *how will I survive in jail?* For he knew jail was a certain eventuality. Anxiety surged through him. His fingers tingled and his breathing quickened. *Will I have my own cell* was followed by *they'll kill me if I don't.* Suffocating images of the gas chamber mixed with an even more terrifying notion of swinging at the end of a rope. The pitch-black expanse beyond the reach of his headlights brought him no solace.

The police were out there.

Jail was out there.

The electric chair was out there.

Eternal damnation was out there.

His breathing sped and his chest spasmed, nearly demanding he pull off the road into the soft gravel. At the height of the panic attack, along the darkest stretch of road since Nebraska, the faint figure of a hitchhiker flickered into view.

"What the hell?" he muttered aloud.

He jammed his foot on the accelerator and the engine raced. *That guy's crazy. Out here this late in the dark.*

The hitchhiker came into the full light as the truck drew abreast. *He's got to be an escapee or a murderer, or...*

The driver shot a glance at the hitchhiker. Even in the harsh glare of the headlights the man's eyes showed a longing to be anywhere other than where he was.

The driver cursed at himself. Completely against his better judgment he slammed on his brakes. The new-technology ABS brought the heavily-laden Volvo to a halt without incident.

The hitchhiker lowered his thumb and sprinted for the truck. When the door opened, he struggled to catch his breath, at the same time attempting a cheery smile. "Going as far as LA?"

The destination caught the driver off-guard—it was his intended terminus. He shook his head at his own poor reasoning. "Get in, sit down, and mind your own damned business."

The hitchhiker stepped onto the running-board, grabbed the hand-hold, and pulled himself inside. The truck slowly accelerated as the driver went through the gears. The rider settled in and an unwitting silence fell over them. Neither man acknowledged it, yet neither man did anything to end it.

After an hour or so, the rider broke the unwritten agreement. "If you don't mind me asking, why'd you pick me up? It sounded like you gunned the engine."

"I'm sitting here trying to figure that out myself."

"You looking for a stranger to answer a question for you, perhaps a question you wouldn't ask of someone familiar?"

Waddy shrugged. "Something like that, I'd reckon."

"You want me to try and figure out what the question is, or do you just want to ask it?"

They drove on for miles in silence. Both the answer and the question remained at bay in the darkness. Finally, the driver exhaled. His words came in a blurt, the nerves behind them obvious. "Ever killed anyone?"

The rider sat up, subconsciously sliding toward the door. "Well, now," he replied with a nervous chuckle. "There's a doozy to start a conversation."

The cab dissolved into a menacing silence, both men waiting for the other's next move.

"Metaphorically or literally?" the rider asked.

The driver immediately clammed up, mad at himself for revealing so much information.

The rider's eyes flicked back and forth between the danger to his left and freedom to his right. His brain raced to calculate the damage to his body if he leapt from a vehicle going sixty miles an hour. The raised height of the cab would surely add to the carnage. Despite the climate-controlled atmosphere of the truck's cab, sweat beaded on his upper lip.

The driver cleared his throat, yet his voice still squeaked as he attempted to stem the damage of his foolish question. "Speaking in the hypothetical, obviously."

The raw awkwardness of the attempt to hide behind the theoretical nature of the question only heightened the rider's angst. He paused before answering and the tension reached a palpable density.

Suddenly, a yellow road sign came into view indicating a sharp left turn. The driver put his hand on the gear shift knob and downshifted into the apex. Clumsily, the rider lost his balance, slid toward the driver, and flailed about to catch himself. In the confusion, his left hand brushed against the exposed skin of the driver's right hand.

Instantly, the rider sat up, completely under control. A look of peace appeared on his face.

The driver flinched at the contact and his rider's klutzy behavior. "What the hell was that all about?"

"You don't want to kill me," the rider chuckled. "You simply want a set of ears to listen to your troubles."

The driver shifted in his custom-made seat, glaring at the chuckling hitchhiker. "Of course, I don't want to kill you, stupid. Is that what you were thinking this whole time?"

"Can't say the thought didn't cross my mind. I'm not in the mood to die today."

The driver made a show of tightening his grip on the big steering wheel. "I'll do my best to keep you alive."

The silence returned; however, the menace had relaxed to amenity.

After a time, the driver eyed his rider. "What did you do to my hand?"

The rider returned the gaze, but didn't speak. He stared out the window into the vast abyss of space. After a time, they passed into a high-mountain tunnel, the interior lights bringing life to the hard-stone walls of the man-made marvel. The brightness stung their eyes and their pupils contracted wildly to accept the brilliance. The passenger realized the belly of the mountain was the first real thing he'd seen besides darkness for over six hours.

His desire for interaction overcame his need for silence. "I read your thoughts."

His nonchalance caught the driver off guard. His eyes snapped to his passenger.

"Don't worry, I'm not messing with you. It's true, I read your thoughts."

"Which ones?"

"I only wanted to know if you were dangerous, so I didn't go back very far."

The driver's eyebrows narrowed. "You're full of shit."

"Whatever you say, Waddy."

The truck jerked with the driver's reaction. "How the hell—?" The driver looked around the cab. "You read my registration card."

"Would that tell me your life's dream is to own an ice cream shop?"

The driver's jaw clenched. "Nice guess."

"Your dad went by the name Worthy Honeycutt."

The driver's eyes widened.

"Don't worry. I couldn't care less about all that. The past is the past. I just want a safe ride, nothing more."

The driver's shoulders relaxed and his eyes returned to the road. "Were you born with that ability?"

The rider shook his head slowly, as if weighed down by copious lament and derision. "No, it was a coming-of-age present from a humorless god."

They rode in silence until the passenger posed a question. "Did your father actually tell people to call him Worthy."

"He was a big man around Denton, Texas." The right-side of the driver's upper lip rose ruefully. "When he used to get mad, he'd call me Unworthy."

"What an asshole."

Both sides of the driver's mouth formed a smile. "My mother hated it when he used that insult."

"Well, from what I saw," the rider mused. "He got what he deserved."

"No one deserves a death so gruesome."

"Yeah, well…" Silence descended on them once again. By force of habit, the passenger glanced at his watch, only then remembering he'd left it in the bedroom of a redhead in Chattanooga—his haste imperative due to her husband returning a day early from a business trip. He smiled to himself. *Yeah, but she was worth a Rolex, let alone my shitty Timex.*

"Done talking?" the driver asked.

The rider faced him. "The answer to your first question is yes."

The driver swallowed hard at the admission. "On purpose or by accident?"

"Accident."

"Accident-accident or were you fighting?"

"I gave a man some advice which didn't turn out well."

"I'd hardly call that murder."

The rider shook his head and turned away. "I knew he'd die if I gave him the information."

"Don't sound like something you'd have any control over."

The rider grimaced. "It didn't matter if he knew or not. He was destined to die in the exact manner I told him. No one has control over destiny."

"That means you, as well."

"I didn't say I had control over it, I just knew what was about to happen. If I hadn't told him, maybe he would have died in peace. Instead, his last moments were filled with terror."

The driver mindlessly drummed his fingers against the wheel. The tune was unimportant, more to buy time than to provide entertainment. "So, what, you can actually tell the future?"

"The short answer is yes."

The driver visibly tensed. "Bullshit!"

The rider chuckled at the naked exclamation and closed his eyes. Once again, they fell into silence. Ten miles further down the highway the truck passed below an illuminated highway sign. The rider's eyes opened.

"Gasoline."

The driver reflexively glanced down at his gauges. "Not yet, I still have a half-tank."

"You used gasoline to kill a man."

The driver's hands squeezed the wheel and his foot stomped on the accelerator. He jerked around in his seat and glared at the passenger. "HOW. THE. HELL. DID. YOU. KNOW. THAT?"

The rider offered a wan smile. "What I know would blow your mind."

"You weren't there! I saw no one and no one saw me!"

"There's no need for me to see anything. I know your memories. I know your dreams." He glanced into the sideview mirror to his right. "I also know you're about to get pulled over."

The driver glanced at his speedometer. It read eighty miles an hour.

A burst of whirling red and blue lights pierced the night behind him. The shrill sound of a siren followed shortly thereafter.

The passenger sat up; his eyes trained on the truck's mirror. "Have you ever seen so many cops?"

GORDO

Al Falcone had it made: money, power, and a beautiful blonde laying nude in his bed. Yet, even the king has to rule. He slid off the silk sheets and got to his feet, shooting his arms to the ceiling to stretch his weary bones.

"Will you be back tonight?"

"Can't doll, I've got dinner with the wife and kids."

"Why won't you spend more time with me, baby. Aren't I pretty enough for you?"

"You're art in watercolor, doll face. Prettiest portrait in the gallery. I've just got too many of 'em hanging on my wall."

"Can't you take a few down and look at only me? You don't need your frumpy old wife; she crimps our style."

Al finished dressing, bent down and kissed her, simultaneously brushing his hand across her breast. "No can do, doll. I made a commitment."

Arms wide, he drew attention to the lavish apartment he kept for her. "Besides, you live in a painting."

When he reached the door, he turned and blew a kiss.

She batted her lavish lashes and purred. "It's hard to appreciate the portrait when you're the Girl in Blue."

The elevator whisked Al directly into the back entrance of the Naso Rotto. He opened the door and strolled into his swank office, past an elaborate four-hundred-gallon aquarium that housed one solitary lionfish of a size unrivaled outside the South Pacific Ocean.

"Yo, Gordo," Al chirped as he went past.

As if on cue, the giant predator turned slowly, eyeing his massive, unreachable quarry. His spiked, venomous rays fully unfurled in preparation for attack.

Spirits buoyed by a morning in the sack with a voluptuous blonde, Al talked to the fish as if he were a close confidant. "Big doings today, Gordo, my boy. Gotta take some money off my lame-ass crew, then I might have to swindle some cash off a local politician or two." Al laughed at his own joke as he opened his desk drawer, removing a snub-nose revolver. He drew out four loose playing cards from the drawer, all aces, and hid them in various places around his clothing.

Uncharacteristically, he kicked off his fine Italian loafers. "Might as well get comfortable. Those bozos are always late."

Al shuffled to a feeder aquarium and netted a large goldfish. He dropped it in Gordo's tank and stood back to watch the fun. Gordo spun to face the frightened fish who struggled for air in the unfamiliar saltwater. In a flash, Gordo charged and inhaled, the inward current drawing his prey into his gaping maw. Scales from the vanquished sacrifice dispersed in a murky cloud.

Al smiled. "Like me with money, gobble it up."

Al began to laugh, reveling in the violence.

"Ah, Gordo, the only one who's got it better than you—"

He checked the gun in his waistband.

"—is me."

THE CONFLUENCE

"For the love of Mike." Waddy Honeycutt whispered the words as a spell against what was to come. "There's something I forgot to tell you."

Joey Ianola's eyes narrowed as a team of State Troopers tactically approached the truck; weapons drawn and pointed at the cab. Both men were extracted at gunpoint and ordered onto the ground. Handcuffs were roughly applied and their bodies were searched. Finally, they were lifted to their feet and taken to a group of well-dressed people near a black sedan parked on the perimeter of the incident.

"What's this all about?" Waddy asked.

A female agent stepped forward and flashed her FBI badge. Her voice both crisp and clear. "We have reason to believe you're operating an interstate racketeering operation, which recently evolved into assault with a deadly weapon and murder."

"Bullshit!" Waddy spat back.

A dark-haired agent stepped forward. Waddy took in the man's confident manner and command presence. *This has got to be the boss.*

"I'm Doug Rawls, Special Agent in Charge," he said. "Were you in Tijeres, New Mexico two days ago?"

"I drive six days a week, I don't remember."

The agent pointed at the broken glass of the sideview mirror and a deep gouge in the front bumper. "Those were made by bullets. Want to reconsider your answer?"

Frustration coursed through Waddy. His face reddened and he began to rage against his handcuffs. Tears streamed down his cheeks.

"You are a mad crybaby," Joey chuckled, as if goading the truck driver.

Waddy kicked at him.

Rawls latched onto Waddy's wrist and stepped between them. Joey had him right where he wanted him. He reached out and grabbed Rawls by the wrist, sealing the connection. All three men's eyes involuntarily closed.

Wanda Tremain drew her weapon, but somehow stayed her hand. Doug Rawls' face showed no signs of pain. She held out her arm, signaling for the surrounding officers to remain in place. That said, her weapon never strayed from Joey Ianola's heart.

The touch of Joey's hand flooded Doug Rawls with images. Not those of Joey's life, but those of Waddy Honeycutt. The original Aqua Velva incident sped by at a million miles an hour, yet as clear and telling as the day it happened. After a period of useless wanderings, Rawls saw the incident in Tijeres, complete with the instigating behavior of the Charles brothers. Nate Hicks followed close behind—his verbal taunts and the admission of involvement in the exact incident for which Waddy was currently detained. Lastly, Rawls caught sight of the faint image of a man with a bushy red beard standing on a box.

"What the—"

Joey released his grip.

Waddy smiled, a contented look covering his face.

Doug Rawls shook visibly, his hands clenched at his side. When he calmed, Rawls opened his eyes and stared at

Joey, struggling to come to grips with what he'd just experienced. He turned and faced the man with whom he'd become so intimate—Wadsworth Hayden Honeycutt III.

Satisfied, Rawls spoke to Wanda Tremain. "These aren't our guys."

"But, Doug…"

"We're looking for a guy by the name of Turk Mullins in downtown Albuquerque. He's the one. Find him and we close the case."

Rawls squared on Joey. "That was a huge chance you took."

"More of a calculated risk."

"As much as it pisses me off that you grabbed me," Rawls smiled. "I want to say thank you. You not only freed an innocent man; you also gave us the information we'll need to get this Mullins asshole off our roadways."

"Do you mind if I ask something," Waddy interjected.

"Go ahead," Rawls replied.

"Who was the woman holding the Shimano Open trophy?"

"You mean, you—" Rawls sputtered.

Joey ran his hand through his hair. "It's omnidirectional."

Rawls gave a humble nod. "She's my soon to be ex-wife."

"Ex-wife?" Wanda Tremain asked.

"Yes, she called when we were staging for the arrest. She wants a divorce."

Joey averted his gaze. The by-product of seeing into a man's future was watching him suffer for his past decisions. The elation of freeing Waddy was suddenly erased by the remorse he felt for a man whose life was now in tatters.

"I love my truck," Waddy said. "But I'd trade it straight-up for a woman like that. She can flat-out fish. What a future!"

"Yes, just not with me." Rawls grew serious, his mind focusing back on the one thing he loved above all else—his job. "Mister Honeycutt, if what I saw is correct, you've personally killed half of the Mullins' gang."

"In self-defense," Joey added.

"Obviously, or you'd still be wearing cuffs." Rawls nodded emphatically. "Now, back to what I was saying; Mullins is going to want you dead. I suggest you come with us for a while for safety reasons."

"What about my truck?"

"We'll take care of it for you."

Waddy wrung his hands in thought. "I don't know about this. Exactly how would—"

Doug Rawls and Waddy Honeycutt negotiated the terms of his surrender in less than five minutes. Waddy needed a break, as did his nerves. Doug Rawls was more than happy to accommodate him, seeing as how he'd just helped solve a three-year old case. When they'd finished, Rawls excused himself to supervise the scene. Wanda Tremain stepped in and began making arrangements for Waddy's entry into the witness protection program.

As they started for the black sedan, Waddy snapped to his senses. *I need to thank the mind-reader.* He turned back to the waning crowd in search of the man who'd saved his life.

Joey Ianola was nowhere to be seen.

I'm Retired

The man pulled up the collar of his shabby black leather jacket against the wind and ducked down a dark alley. His skin sharp from the cold, his mind muddled from the hum of voices in his head, he lit a cigarette and began counting his steps as a distraction.

"Hey, Buddy."

The man turned his attention to a bum seated on the back steps of a boarded-up business; barely visible in the ambient light of a large neon sign atop a nearby hotel.

"Yeah?"

"Got another one of those?" The bum pointed at his Marlboro.

The man's jaw tightened, then softened suddenly. He stared at the stranger and handed him a cigarette.

"Thanks," the bum replied. "I thought you were going to say no for a second."

"Maybe."

"What changed your mind?"

The man's eyes squinted in the gloom. "You have a perfect golden aura."

The bum sat up; a smile adorned his face. "You have the sight?"

"Unfortunately."

The bum's forehead creased. "Unfortunately?"

"That's what I said."

The bum beckoned him forward with the wave of his hand. "Come into the light."

Reluctantly, the man stepped into the glow of flickering neon.

The bum nodded his head. "Your aura has dimmed to a pale gray. Why's that?"

"It's a long story."

The bum picked up a Styrofoam container of moldy Chinese food and began to eat with his fingers. "Do I look like I have anything but time?'

The man thought of the bum's golden hue. *Something's afoot.* He pulled up a rickety chair and sat. "I hear voices."

The bum shrugged his shoulders. "Doesn't everyone who has the gift of sight?'

"Well—"

The bum extended his hand. "Call me Sid."

The man took it without hesitation. "I'm Joe."

"You look like a Joey to me."

"Most people call me Joey."

"Is this why your story's so long? The introductions?"

Joey smiled. "I wasn't born with the gift of sight, it just kind of happened."

"Few are," Sid replied. "Many of us spend our entire lives in search of it. Did you buy it at a joke shop on Fifth Avenue?"

"I wish it was so simple," Joey smiled. "Truth is I was struck by lightning."

"Ah, the Ben Franklin trick. Did it hurt?"

"Oh, yeah. Like a son-of-a-bitch."

Sid's eyes softened. "What happened?"

"Once I woke up, I could see other people's thoughts, see reincarnated souls, pick out the colors of people's auras, and—" Joey hesitated.

"And?"

"I don't normally tell people this shit."

"And?" Sid repeated.

"Sometimes I can regenerate life."

"Impressive," Sid replied. "I'm not sure I'd want that one."

"It only works on small animals and insects."

"Party tricks for the non-believers?"

"A believer would be the last one I'd show. I'm not sure the Jesus set would appreciate reanimation."

"Jesus, huh. What's he accomplished since taking over the family business?" Sid joked.

Joey couldn't help but chuckle.

"You keep that gift hidden?" Sid asked.

"No one's ever seen me do it. I don't want the questions, or the attention."

Sid offered a knowing nod. "Adept at avoiding crowds?"

"Lately I've been avoiding people all-together."

Sid shrugged. "I used to pull the same trick; months alone with my own thoughts. It's refreshing sometimes, but mostly we need human interaction."

"Why?"

"To remind ourselves we're doing just fine. There's a lot of people worse off than either one of us."

Joey glanced around at the dingy surroundings.

Sid cut him off before he could speak. "Where one's physical body resides has absolutely zero correlation to their spiritual health. A man can be equally as enlightened here as in a golden temple. No?"

"Good thing," Joey cracked.

"Says a man covered in coal dust? I'd wager you've been hopping trains for solitude?"

Joey's eyes narrowed.

"Pickled with alcohol to drown the voices?" Sid added.

"How did you—"

"Come on," Sid said. "You're not the only one in this alley with gifts."

Joey thought of the bottle in his pack. "Dark and lonely are the times of men, I guess."

"I've never been one for liquid detachment," Sid shrugged. "I detest the loss of control."

"Loss of control?"

Sid nodded. "Liquor either makes people very talkative or unreasonably quiet, usually contrary to their normal behavior. I enjoy who I am, so I don't take direction from outside sources."

"It usually makes me melancholy."

"I'd hazard a guess everything makes you melancholy, hence the gray aura."

Joey's eyes widened. "I simply don't have a lot to say."

"You can tell a lot about the quality of a man by the stories he tells. Men who haven't done much tell the wildest stories. Men who have seen too much, speak little."

"Have you seen too much?" Joey asked.

The bum sat forward, bringing his face into sharp relief. The stories of a thousand lifetimes rested upon his wrinkles. "Luckily, time is also the thief of memories, both good and bad. I sleep well, if that's your question."

Joey's eyes narrowed. "Wait, exactly how old are you?"

Sid grinned. "In this life, or in total?"

Joey's mind raced. *The gift of sight. The wisdom of a sage. Sid.* "You're the Buddha."

The grin grew into a smile. "Somewhere in my past."

Joey stood. "You're practically a god. Why are you here in this shitty alley? Why are you wasting your life? Why aren't you out helping people?"

Sid's brow furrowed. "So many questions; so little time allowed for answers. First off, I have many more lives to live, thank you very much. Secondly, it seems as though I remember that whatever I do is my choice. I don't recall having to run it by you."

Joey sat down as if slapped. "Of course, of course. I apologize. Please, forgive me."

Sid dismissed him with a wave of his hand. "Wrong religion, Joe. I'm not in the forgiveness business."

It was Joey's turn to smile. "Touché."

Sid looked around at his grim surroundings. "Why am I here? Let me try to explain it in modern terms so you can understand. Each life is like a highway. Some people lack imagination, or confidence, so they seek a form of safety on the wide, concrete Interstates that constitute our accepted institutions. There are great big signs telling them where to go, plus how and when to get there; reassuring them that the wisdom of the crowd will show them the correct route. They never even chance a peek at the exit ramps along the way, disregarding those opportunities to chart their own map. Included among them, there are those who drive only in the fast lane, blinking their lights for others to get out of their way. They expect everyone to follow their lead without deviation. You know who I'm talking about—religious leaders, politicians, etcetera. They look behind them expecting to see the freeway packed with followers."

Sid spat on the ground. "Boring!" He took a deep drag on his cigarette. "Me, I like to get off the main route and walk dirt roads meandering beside a slow-moving river. Who knows, I may eventually end up in the same place as those who've removed the blinkers from their vehicle, but if I do, I will arrive at my destination by *my* choice. I will have seen the rich tapestry of the world, not simply the monotonous concrete rushing by at ninety miles an hour."

He looked around the dreary alley and smiled. "Right now, I've simply pulled into a rundown rest stop for a spiritual nap."

"Can you give me directions? For my own path, I mean."

"Your path is yours alone, Joey. If I tell you the way, it is my path, not yours."

Joey's eyes dropped and his face went slack.

"Like I told you on the steps of the Amarillo train station—stay in the light."

Joey's eyes shot open. "Wait, that was you? Why didn't you…"

"I have gifts of my own," Sid said. "You can't read me as well as you can others, plus you weren't ready to listen then, and perhaps you still aren't, but…" Sid took one last drag and flicked the cigarette butt into the shadows. "I will give you one small bit of advice."

Joey looked up; his face filled with longing.

Sid locked eyes with the young seer. "Enjoy the ride, and never go so fast you miss the exit signs."

"It seems as though the last couple of years I've been trying to tunnel my way through life."

"Tunnels are dark and lonely places, Joey. Plus, it's hard to see what's around when your life is spent in the underground darkness."

Joey smiled as understanding eased his countenance. "You speak in riddles, old man, but I get what you're saying."

He offered Sid another cigarette. "Stay in the light. With the burden of *knowing*, well, that's an easy thought to forget."

"So are the days of the week if one tries."

Joey scooted closer, admiring the golden hue surrounding Sid's persona. "Have you actually been around since four-hundred BC?"

"Oh, no," Sid replied.

Joey nodded at the silliness of his question.

"I've been around since way before then."

Joey swallowed hard. "Are you immortal?"

"That's a tricky question, Joey. I've had the same soul since I first achieved enlightenment. I've lived and died many times, and I've burned through more bodies than I care to remember. But, every time I'm reborn, my gathered wisdom is redeemed."

"You remember everything you've learned since before Christ was born?"

Sid smiled. "Jesus was a pure soul, but Confucius is the one they quote in cookies."

Joey laughed, then grew serious. "Why haven't you made yourself known again? To help, I mean?"

"Oh goodness, no—I'm retired. The world can heal itself without me."

Joey fixed the Buddha with a stare. "Is there hope for us?"

"I think the correct way to phrase the question is, 'should I hold on to hope?'"

"Well?"

"Never lose hope, Joey. The hope for all mankind is held in the hope within each soul."

The hotel's neon lamp flickered. Joey squinted to keep Sid in sight. "For hope, I need faith, and mine is—"

"You're a good man, Joey. Good enough to be handed this huge responsibility. Run as you may, but you'll never outrun the obligation of the gift. It might take a few lives for you to grow comfortable, but you will. Trust me, you will."

"You mean I'll have more lives?" The muscles in Joey's jaw clenched. "But I don't want that burden!"

"Listen to me, Joey; if one is to live forever, they'd best love themselves, for all others will eventually die. Stay in the light, Joey."

The hotel's neon lamp faltered, plunging the alley into total darkness.

111

"Sid?" Joey felt around the stoop for the bum.

"As I told you at the Amarillo train station—keep moving forward, everything else is death."

"I still can't believe that was you."

"It's always been me." Sid's voice cut through the inky black. "Like I said, you're not the only one with gifts."

"Please, stay! I need your guidance! The voices, they—"

"Use them for good, like you did when you saved the kid. It's the only path to peace."

"But, Sid, please...I..."

The neon light flickered back on, dimly lighting the alley. Joey searched the area, but Sid was nowhere to be found. He sat down and replayed the discussion over in his head.

Sid looked down upon the man in the alley, hope filling his breast. He spoke, yet no voice was heard. *Keep moving forward, Joey. Stay in the light. It's the only path to peace.*

Joey mustered a smile at the thought.

THE BARFLY

The joint looked a hundred years old. You know the one, every city has a bar like this—dirty on the outside, worse on the inside. It's usually on the corner of Sixth and Loneliness, with a fading neon sign blinking its name—*The Rendezvous*, or something similar. No one knows it exists, except for those chosen few who consider it home. Each stool tells a story, which if collected would engender more heartaches and tears than any soap opera ever written. The bartender could be Ebenezer Anybody: tall and thin with droopy eyes, short and round with a frying pan face—no matter; it's not who is serving the drinks that draws them in. The only necessity is a set of sympathetic ears.

It just so happens tonight is Vince Dolan's turn with the dirty dishrag and cynical smile. Fourth night of his five-night week. One-thirty loomed close—he could tell the hour by the barking of his dogs. The place was almost empty and smelled of spilled beer, dried sweat, and desperation. Vince lamented the meager tidings in his tip jar. *Barely enough to cover my gas home.* He poured himself a jigger of the cheap stuff, watered it down, and drank it in one gulp. *The boss'll never miss it.*

The glow of a cigarette drew his attention. Vince flinched, as no one had been sitting there a minute ago. "There's no smoking in here, mister."

The man leaned forward and put his elbows on the bar, his face coming out of the shadows. Dark circles framed the barfly's intense eyes. "Jameson's, rocks."

"You'll need to put that out first."

The barfly's hand moved in a flash—the cigarette was gone.

"What the—" the bartender muttered.

"Jameson's, rocks," the barfly's cement-mixer voice repeated.

Vince pulled his eyes away and reached for the bottle of whiskey.

114

"Not that," the barfly spat. "The good stuff."

Vince reached one shelf higher for the 18-Year-Old Limited Reserve, curiosity setting in. He glanced from the corner of his eye, taking in the barfly's black leather jacket and dark watchman's cap. *Probably a dock worker.* He finished pouring and turned in time to see the barfly's hand burst forward, snatching an object from the smoky air. His massive mitt contracted, then dropped a crushed housefly onto the dingy wooden surface. Its bent wings and flattened body lay still in the streaks of the dirty dishrag's grimy residue.

"Don't put that thing there," Vince barked. "I just cleaned."

The barfly extended his right index finger and touched the fly, never losing contact. After a few seconds, its wings fluttered, then began to beat in earnest. The fly rose like a wobbly drunk in an alley and disappeared back into the shadows.

Vince Dolan's eyes widened. "Hey, I know you, I've seen you on the news."

"Jameson's."

Vince dropped two ice cubes into the glass. "You're famous."

"Infamous."

"Yeah, I suppose." Vince slid him the glass. "But you made a big stack as I remember."

"Money, I've got." The barfly drew a thick roll from the pocket of his leather jacket, slapping a fifty on the bar.

"Thanks, mister. Joey something, right?"

"Joey Ianola."

"Yeah, that's it." Vince leaned back and crossed his arms. "I haven't heard of you in quite some time, like you dropped off the face of the earth. Where've you been?"

"I got tired of reporters watching my every move, trying to catch something remarkable on film. They wanted a messiah." Joey's eyes rose slowly. "I'm no messiah. I'm just some bum who got hit by lightning."

"If you don't mind me saying, Joey, I never read about you being a bum. All the stuff I read was in your favor."

"They always write good stuff when the wave is cresting. All the while they're searching your closets for skeletons to use against you when the wave crashes onto the shore. The press enjoys a feel-good story, but they love a failed hero even more."

116

"True, that. So, where've you been in the meantime? And how in the hell did you end up in a dive bar in the middle of Shitsville, USA?"

"What's your name?"

"Vince Dolan."

"You want the long version or the short, Vince?"

"Nobody's here but us, so give me the long."

Joey held out his right index finger. The tip bent sharply toward his thumb; its discolored skin both slick and shiny. "This is where it all started."

"The lightning?"

"Yeah, the lightning. I was fourteen, freshman year of high school." Joey paused. "I swear, every time I tell this story, it seems like yesterday. Typical rainy day in Brooklyn. My friends and I hiked down Erskine Street to where it dead-ends at Jamaica Bay. We were smoking, talking crap—you know; big, tough high schoolers. Too stupid to even get out of the rain. One of the clouds reminded me of my Aunt Ruby's poodle. I pointed at it to show my pals—next thing I remember is waking up six months later in a hospital room."

"Six months, wow. A lotta stuff can change in six months."

"My mom's voice brought me out of it. I heard her yell at my dad, 'Jim, his eyes, they're open!' I saw my old man's face, so I reached up and touched him. That's when it started."

"The Gift?"

"Some call it that."

"You don't?"

"If all of a sudden you could see people's thoughts, see their futures, know if their souls had walked the earth in a previous form—would you call it a gift?"

Vince's eyes grew hungry at the question. "If it made me rich, famous even, I'd take the chance."

"Even if the first thing you saw was your dad's skanky mistress? His thefts from work? His memories of beating your mom? Or, to know he'd be dead in less than eight months? Would you still want it?"

Vince leaned back at the ferocity of the question. "Only you'd be able to answer that, Joey. You're the only one who's ever—"

"The answer always boils down to NO, Vince. It's like living inside both a dream and a nightmare."

"The dream never outweighs the other?"

"Sometimes, in the moment. It's the same as an addiction. The high is life in the clouds, but when reality hits, you wake up in a Shitsville saloon."

"So, it's all bad?"

"No." Joey shook his head slowly. "There's the blind."

"The blind?"

"Yeah, through me they can see what I've experienced. The travel, the exotic locations, the people. I could feel their excitement, their wonder. It's—" Joey went silent, his thoughts a million miles away. "It's an exhilarating, wonderful feeling, Vince. Beyond mere words."

After a time, the bartender's mouth curled into a grin. "Tell me about some of the good times."

"I slept with quite a few women you've seen in the headlines. I made a ton of money off some of the richest people in the world. I met kings, queens, presidents, celebrities—that part was all pretty cool. Famous people flock to oddities; I guess us freaks make their make-believe lives feel normal in some twisted way."

"The lives they must live—" Vince mused.

"Are more messed up and complicated than even they can solve." Joey's face darkened. "For every fun story there's

119

ten that make your skin crawl. Religious nuts calling you a fraud in the press, damning you to the fires of Hell—malicious shit."

"I could see where they'd have a problem with—"

"A problem? Maybe in the public eye, but in private they were some of my best customers. They figured I had a pipeline to Him."

"Do you?"

"A question I've asked Him a million times. I'm still waiting for the answer."

"Are they the worst to deal with, the religious?"

"No, unfortunately, that distinction also belongs to the blind."

"Huh?"

"When their session is over, they know they'll lose the connection to my sight, only to return to the bleak darkness of their own world. The depression. The sadness. It's hard—on them," he drained the whiskey, "and on me."

"I never thought—"

"No one's ever thought of that but me. Although, in the beginning, I never really thought, I just did. Long sessions with people who've lived fantastic lives, with futures to match. Expansive to see, being a simple boy from Brooklyn. It was all a dream. That is, until the first nightmare came along." Joey held out his empty glass.

Vince knew instinctively to fill it. "Bad, huh? The nightmares."

"The first one happened about a month after I started selling sessions. A Hollywood bigwig. Paid me huge bucks—cash—before we even started."

Vince slid the refilled glass in front of him.

Joey took a long sip. "He thought I could only see forward, not back. He had a thing for young boys, forced himself on them."

Vince blanched. "That's sick. What'd you do?"

"Reported him to the police. Unfortunately—" Joey sucked on an ice cube in thought. "Unfortunately, the police can't act unless they have hard evidence. They wouldn't believe me and I never got close enough to the guy again to gather information."

"You saw reality, but they treated it as fiction. That definitely qualifies as a nightmare."

Joey shrugged. "The only positive is I also saw his impending death. One of the victim's dads took care of business."

"Did the dad go to jail for it?"

Joey grinned. "Nah, somehow, someone tipped him off to the next time the asshole would be alone in his mansion. It seems the killer got in and out of the scene undetected."

The bartender grinned. "Almost as if someone could tell the future."

"You see my point, Vince? I helped bring about the monster's destruction, but I also had to see his memories; to feel them, experience them. It took me a long time to get over it."

"That's harsh," Vince said. "But at least you got your money up front."

Silence descended on the room, but not in either man's thoughts. Imagination ran wild, as did memories.

"Is money all you want out of life, Vince?"

"Look, I know money can't buy happiness, but it can buy a lot of things that make you happy."

Joey's eyes focused on his bent finger. "The shortest session I ever had was a Chicago billionaire. The man had the world by the balls; money, women, everything. He arranged a session atop one of his skyscrapers. His past amazing; his future stunted. It only took me two or three seconds to know his end was close. He paid me and I left." Joey glanced up. "He left a

122

few minutes later. The elevator failed and he fell a hundred floors to his death."

"You're making shit up now to prove a point."

"About money not solving anything?"

"Yeah."

"Nah, it happened. It was in the papers."

Vince shrugged; his face resigned. "Yeah, I mighta read about it." He hastily rubbed the counter with the dishrag. After a moment, his eyes open wide and he stopped. "Hey, wait a minute. How come the guy in Chicago didn't see the elevator was messed up? Can't they see the past and the future?'

"Everyone's different. The billionaire had no need to worry about the future, so maybe he didn't bother trying to see it. Dunno, and in the end, don't really care. Like I said, everyone's different."

"Was he the only one?"

"Not even close. I had one lady down in Atlanta who didn't see anything either direction. She had so much money and time on her hands, and had done so many things in her life that she ran out of natural curiosity. Demanded her money back."

"That must have pissed you off, losing out on your cash."

"I told you before, Vince; money ain't everything."

"Yeah, well, maybe not to rich people."

"Listen, with my reputation I could charge a lot, sometimes well over a hundred grand a session. Most of the people I *read* were wealthy. I can tell you without hesitation—money doesn't solve anything. It leads the stupid further into stupidity, and the greedy further into greed. It's an enhancer, not a panacea."

"You could get that much, simply to read the future?"

"Rich people have curiosities same as we do. The difference is, they have the money to satisfy them."

Vince poured himself a drink, absorbing the conversation, mulling it in his mind.

"I never charged them; you know."

Vince looked up. "Who?"

"The blind."

"Nothing?"

"Nothing."

"Why not?"

124

"The feelings, the emotions, the sheer elation of their *seeing* in the moment—it was payment enough."

Vince stared at the barfly, his mind working hard for an angle. "So, you charged the rich outrageously and you gave the blind a pass—kind of like a lightning bolt-powered version of Robin Hood?"

Joey chuckled.

"Did the cops ever use you?" Vince asked.

"A few times, but I started refusing after a while."

"Why?"

"The ugliness, the stress. Crime is a nasty corner of the world."

"But it worked when you tried, huh?"

"Yeah, I put several high-profile bad people behind bars."

"Was the money big in that racket?"

"Nah, expenses mostly."

"Wow, the government seems like a big lamb to fleece."

"There you go with the money again," Joey snapped.

"What, you don't like money?"

"Sure. I made more, and spent more than any ten men. But, money's just a vehicle."

"A long, black Cadillac with 24-carat door handles, maybe?"

"Sometimes, and sometimes it's a horse-drawn hearse. False people living false lives—the self-destruction, addictions, overdoses, suicides."

"Wow, you can be a downer, Joey."

"I didn't ask for a freaking lightning bolt to change my entire world, Vince. I'd rather dig ditches in Peoria."

The bartender kneaded the dirty dishrag in thought, then mumbled. "Say, maybe you could read me?"

"To quote an old friend, I'm retired."

"Come on, Joey. Just one more—for old time's sake."

"You sure you want to know?"

"Yeah, what could go wrong? I'm already stuck in this shithole."

"And how do you propose to meet my usual fee?"

"Damn, I didn't think of that. I don't have much. This ain't even my bar. I could give you what's left in the Jameson bottle."

An avalanche of fresh cubes cascaded into the bin of the nearby ice machine, momentarily distracting the barfly. He took off the watchman's cap and rubbed his fingers through his hair. "Ah, why not. I've got nothing else going on."

Vince grinned and threw the dishrag onto the dirty counter. He leaned forward and Joey touched his right index finger to the bartender's temple. Vince's eyes flashed, his face contorting in the agony and ecstasy of memory and visions. When Joey pulled away, the bartender's eyes were filled with tears.

Joey took out his wad of money, peeled off half and placed it on the bar. "You keep it, Vinny. Go home and enjoy the time you have left."

Sobs filled the room. Joey rose and started toward the door. When his hand grasped the handle, Vince cried out. "Please, Joey, please. Is there anything I can do?"

"If I were you, Vinny, I'd avoid elevators."

THE CONFLUENCE, SCENA DUE

Vince Dolan stared at himself in the mirror behind the bar. His eyes were red from crying and his cheeks flushed. A million disparate thoughts ran through his head, but the vision he'd seen when Joey Ianola touched his temple dominated all others.

"I'm going to die," he mumbled to his reflection.

The image of an elevator stuck in his mind like a scene on a broken television.

He shook his head and focused on his own eyes staring back at him. "This is all Al Falcone's doing. He put me in this spot."

He picked up the phone, thinking of a call to the Bayonne branch of the Mafia, but thought better of it. "There's only one thing to do." He took a semi-automatic .22 out of its hiding place beneath the bar. "Someone's gotta die." He stuffed the gun in the waistband of his work pants. "It might as well be me who does it."

He marched across the room, flung open the door, flipped the sign to "closed," and stomped down the steps into the cool night air.

At that exact moment, Lefty Salducci, Knuckles Pecota, and Specks Johansen entered the Naso Rotto, acknowledged Al Falcone, and made their way inside the main room.

Lefty went behind the bar and poured himself a shot of tequila, downed it in one gulp, then poured himself another. Knuckles went straight to the card table and made small talk with the boss. He flipped on the television adjacent to the bar and tuned in the local news.

Specks planted himself in front of the aquarium, admiring the marvelous beauty of the massive lionfish who elegantly dominated his domain. *What I wouldn't give to have your power, Gordo. To be king of my own universe.*

Al sat at the gaming table. "Let's do this."

The others gathered reluctantly, knowing their pockets were about to be picked.

Vince Dolan let himself into the back door of the Naso Rotto building with a key he'd lifted when Al was out of town. He reached into his waistband and drew out the .22.

Al was behind the next door, unaware of Vince's presence. He'd be easy to surprise.

Knuckles was behind the same door. The big enforcer would also have to die.

Lefty was behind the door—dangerous and constantly on guard. He'd be hardest to kill.

Specks was behind the door, nothing but a mealy-mouthed worm. He'd be last to die.

Vince took a deep breath to calm himself, thinking of what he was about to do. *I don't want to kill anyone, but…*

He thrust the barrel of the .22 out in front of him—and pushed the elevator button for the roof.

Knuckles started off winning—big. His money troubles seemed far behind him. The enforcer imagined dropping a wad of cash on the dining room table at home, shutting his wife's mouth if even for one brief second. Specks held his own, easing his worries about the cheating rat who was his boss. He figured as

131

long as he broke even it was a victory. *Money saved is money earned.* Lefty simply drank himself stupid. His chip stack fluctuated, the occasional win being a product of intoxication-driven bravado. He could care less, after all, the booze was free.

Vince arrived on the roof at the same time Lefty spotted the ace in Al's left sleeve.

Lefty let it slide.

Vince couldn't. He stared out at the beautiful skyline of the city, feeling no connection to anything, or anyone, before him. He began to weep softly, lamenting a life lived so haphazardly, with no direction other than the wrong one. He climbed onto the ledge.

Knuckles felt only mild concern when his luck took a subtle downturn. Three hands later he panicked. Gone was the money for a new sofa. Gone was the money for his kid's braces. One hand later, all his money vanished. The only thing remaining were thoughts of the diatribe his wife held for him when he got home.

Al's eyes darted back and forth between the crew, watching for clues of discovery. None seen, he grinned like a man who'd won the lottery.

Vince took out his phone, hit "record video," and turned the lens on himself. He took a steadying breath and spoke in a droll monotone. "I have no life, thanks to Al Falcone. I have no future, thanks to Joey Ianola. I'm dead anyway you look at it."

He put the .22 in his mouth and pulled the trigger.

Vince landed at the same time Knuckles saw the ace in Al's back pocket.

"Somebody's cheating," the big man rumbled.

In the ruckus, they never heard the body slam into the concrete outside.

The police were never far from the Naso Rotto, as the club's shady clientele made it a target-rich environment for arrests. The area beat cop responded to a radio call of a jumper and arrived on the scene in less than a minute. A crowd gathered quickly and more officers arrived to assist with the investigation.

No one noticed when a man in a black leather jacket dipped under the crime scene tape and disappeared inside the club. His only reaction to the broken body on the sidewalk was a forlorn shake of his head.

Al stood when he heard the front door open, extending his hands out to his enraged enforcer. "Calm down, Knucks. It's a card from an old deck. No one's cheating here."

Knuckles was too afraid to push the subject.

Lefty was too drunk to care.

Specks already knew Al was a cheater. He shrugged and returned to his cards.

"Anybody here?' Joey called.

Al stepped into the empty main room. "Yeah, what can I do for you?"

Joey grinned. "A friend told me I could find a game here." He took out his remaining bundle of cash and held it out for Al to see.

Two of Al's basic needs came into play; survival and profit. *New blood will distract Knuckles and I could use the green in the new guy's hand.* "Sure, come on over."

134

The game recommenced with Al employing a syrupy charm to welcome the visitor.

The senior detective at the crime scene had no intention of climbing stairs in search of evidence. He grabbed a rookie patrolman to do it for him. "Go to the roof and find out whatever you can about this guy. Look for scuffmarks on the ledge and stuff like that. If you see anything, get on the radio for the forensics guys. Got it?"

The rookie nodded and left in a flash. He hadn't broken a sweat when he reached the roof. Vince's telephone was the first thing he saw. The gun being the second.

It wasn't long before Al started winning big—again. Emboldened by the new player at the table, Knuckles called foul—again.

"Someone's cheating!"

Al stood. Behind Knuckles, he saw a picture of Vince on the television. The crawl read: Local man jumps to his death.

The perfect diversion.

"Hey, look, Vince is on the tube." The three goons looked.

Joey didn't bother. He already knew what was about to go down.

"Ah, too bad," Knuckles said. "I really liked him."

"The fucker owed me money," Al added. He cringed when his own face came on screen. "Hey, what the—"

Joey's face followed immediately; his name featured prominently below it.

Al pointed directly at him. "Hey, that's you!"

Joey stood, raised his hands to his side, and his eyes rolled back in their sockets.

"In this room is the person who will cause your death."

All four gangsters drew their weapons, pointing them at the seer.

"One of you has practiced deceit on his friends."

Three guns shifted to Al.

"One of you will feel the sting of an admired friend."

Knuckles got confused at the declaration and didn't know who to point at. Specks shouted, "What the fuck?"

"You will all die tonight."

All four of the gangster's guns whipped back to Joey. The television showed a group of SWAT members working their way toward the front of the Naso Rotto club.

136

Specks was first to notice. "Look!"

Al took advantage of the distraction. "The cops are a bigger threat to us than we are to ourselves. Put your guns away and act like we didn't see them coming."

Lefty and Knuckles ditched the weapons in their jacket pockets. Specks reluctantly followed suit.

Al laughed to himself. *Suckers!* Lefty was drunk, so he pointed and fired at his next biggest threat—Knuckles.

He missed.

Lefty fell ass-over-tea kettle backwards, landing hard on the cushioned floor. Specks dove for cover under the table, grasping for the gun he'd just put away. Stunned he'd dodged death, Knuckles froze. Al didn't miss the second time. Specks took a shot at Al but missed when Knuckles' lifeless body landed on his legs. Lefty did his job, taking out the threat to his boss with a casual shot to the accountant's temple. Not even bothering to thank his friend for watching his back, Al took a hasty shot at the hitman, which struck the table above his head. That snapped Lefty out of his fog—partly. He shot at Al as the boss ran for safety. The bullet went wide and smashed into the aquarium glass. Four-hundred gallons of saltwater exploded onto the floor.

As did one cantankerous lionfish.

In his race to freedom, Al didn't see his old pal Gordo. His stockinged left foot landed hard on the fish's extended barbs, driving one sharply through his skin. He went down in a cavalcade of screams. A lonely ace tumbled to the floor beside him.

Lefty scrambled to his feet and stumbled through the pond of brackish muck.

Joey rose from the table. "There's my cue." He disappeared out the back door.

Lefty stood over his boss, who squirmed in pain. The ace caught his eye. "You fucking cheater. You tried to kill me." He pointed his gun at Al's miniscule heart.

The front door burst open and the lead SWAT cop raised his automatic weapon at the hitman. "Drop the gun!"

"Fuck you!" he screamed as he pulled the trigger. Al's body went slack.

The first barrage of .40 caliber ammo hit Lefty in the chest. The last hit him square between the eyes.

EVERYTHING OLD BEGINS ANEW

As the eastbound freight train picked up speed, Joey Ianola
sprinted across a set of unused tracks and latched onto the ladder
of a nearly-empty gondola carrying scrap-steel rebar. He swung
his backpack over the side and climbed aboard, ducking down to
hide from any prying eyes of the railyard bulls. Sweat stained
his shirt, so he took it off. He put his naked back against the hot,
rusted-iron bed and watched the edges of the city pass by—the
buildings slowly shrinking in both size and frequency.

I'm never coming back here, he thought. *I don't want to
go through this shit again.*

When the train crossed the trestles, indicating they were
over the river, he knew they'd be in rural farmland within
minutes. The humidity eased—barely.

Joey exhaled, and shook out his hands. *Less people means less voices.* He opened his backpack and withdrew a forty-ounce beer. He glanced westward over the edge of the car toward the setting sun, glad to be moving east. As the day waned toward dusk, he laid his damp shirt over his aching legs. The first spike of distant lightning caught him by surprise. The ensuing rumble of thunder further darkened his mood.

We're heading right toward it.

He took a long draw off the bottle and closed his eyes.

Where are you going, Joe? You're most definitely not following Sid's advice. He took another gulp, allowing it to linger on his tongue. Memories of his short stay in the big city played over in his mind.

His encounter with the ravenous press: *Even when I do what's right, it goes wrong.*

The destruction of Doug Rawls' marriage. *The poor sap.*

And Vince. He swallowed the beer in his mouth. *Ah, Vinny, you fool.*

He did his best to move on, but the memory of the bartender persisted. *You shouldn't have showed him.*

"But, he begged," he mumbled to himself.

You should have let him live his last days in peace.

140

"But he begged."

So, that's going to become my mantra? Excusing myself because someone begged for their own future? You're nothing but bad luck, Joey.

No, I'm not.

Waddy came to mind. He recalled the last scene of the truck driver's future flashing through his mind during the clench with Agent Rawls. A single-story ice cream parlor in downtown Littleton, Colorado. The perfect spot for a witness protection hideout. The sign over the entrance read, Shorty's Sweets. A tiny man with a bushy red beard and a white ten-gallon hat climbed onto a wooden box hidden from view behind the counter, his last words spoken with sheer joy: "You want sprinkles with that?"

Joey grinned. *Waddy got his happy ending.* His face darkened. *Why not me?*

Joey threw the empty bottle over the side and took out another. The edges of his mind grayed from the strong brew. *Exactly what Sid said, pickled by alcohol.*

The conversation with the retired Buddha rushed back to him.

"Stay in the light, Joey."

Shit, I can't even see the light anymore.

"It's the only path to peace."

There's no such thing in my life.

Another snippet of the conversation bit him hard. *Life—or lives.* Joey shuddered. *I can't imagine having to live through this as many times as Sid has. The poor bastard.*

Another spike of lightning lit up the night. Joey saw his hands, remembering he hadn't opened the second beer. In the humidity, it had grown tepid. The ensuing thunder ushered in a spattering of rain. Joey grabbed up his belongings and scrambled from the open-air car to the relative safety of a hidey-hole on a grain hauler. He guzzled the second forty-ouncer with minimal pauses for air. His belch resounded in the metal cubby.

Another bolt of lightning flashed across the horizon. *Metal? I wonder what would happen if one of those hit this train.* The thunder rolled—louder—the interval between it and the lightning shorter. The rain thickened and the sweetness of the ionized air filled Joey's nostrils.

We're getting closer.

His offhand question came back to him.

What would happen if we were struck? His mind raced. *It'd send a jolt clear through this giant hunk of steel.*

The beer slowed his reasoning, but he clung to the thought. *I wonder if I would reset?* His heart quickened. *If the voices would stop?*

The sky lit up, the thundercrack followed almost immediately.

I survived once and it ruined my life. Would a second strike give me freedom?

He climbed out of the cubby, perching himself on the rail. The heavy rain pelted his face. A bolt of lightning flashed. Joey surveyed the terrain in an instant. *Flat, barren farmland.* Thunder crashed again. *We're square in the middle of it.* The train jerked, picking up speed to outrun the worst of the storm.

Joey bent and picked up a six-foot length of metal rebar.

Another bolt of lightning accompanied by simultaneous thunder.

They're coming faster now.

Another bolt flashed from the rumbling clouds. Joey raised his eyes to the black sky, rain pelting his face.

Crack—boom!

Nothing to be seen for miles.

Sage words came back to him from the conversation he had with the Buddha in the dingy alley. "Never lose hope, Joey. The hope for all mankind is held in the hope within each soul."

Fuck this shit! I don't have any hope but this.

Joey leapt from the train, slammed hard against the gravel pad of the tracks, and rolled to a stop in a drainage ditch. The pain drove out the alcohol cobwebs. In its place, the voices began screaming in his ears.

A bolt of lightning lit up the horizon. Joey grabbed the rebar and scrambled to level land.

What would happen?

He stepped over a low, barbed-wire fence and marched into the field.

It's time to find out.

Joey extended the thin rebar skyward, the cuts on his arms made by the rocks stung in the humidity. He turned his face to the heavens as the voices screamed bloody murder.

No, Joe, no, resonated between his ears. *Don't do it!*

"Shut the fuck up!" Joey cackled.

****

"Push!" the doctor urged.

The woman took a shallow, quick breath, her face a mask of determination. She squeezed her husband's hand and pushed with all her might. His face widened in a smile.

"It's coming, honey. Push!"

Another sharp breath, another exertion. Her husband pulled the surgical mask off his smiling face. "It's a boy!"

The doctor laid the slime-covered baby on her chest. Tears filled her eyes at the beauty of what they'd created. The baby squinted at her through its barely opened eyes. Miraculously, it reached out its hand, laying its fingers on her cheek.

Memories poured through her skin, flooding the baby's brain—her future followed close behind.

The baby's mind roared to life with knowledge unsuited for its newborn age.

I'm back where I started.

As his mother pulled him close, the baby began to scream.

THE END

Acknowledgments

As always, a HUGE thank you goes out to the members of the Lyons' Den Writing Group. This book would not have been possible without the input and wisdom of Sir William Lyons III, Toni Floyd, Gordon Lazarus, and Tom Tucker.

Another HUGE thank you goes out to my wife, Lynn for her valued assistance in reading and editing this manuscript. I love you!

As always, this is for my family: Lynn and Elizabeth. You are my inspiration!

Last, and certainly not least, THANK YOU to those precious friends who have read and commented on my previous books. I'm so glad you enjoy them!

If You Enjoyed The Barfly & Other Oddities
by Big John McKenzie

You may also enjoy the adventures of:
Marshal Milo Thorne, Frontier Philosopher

In case you missed them, the first three books of the series;
The Crooked Trail, Bloodshot Sunset, and Halo Or Horns
are available through Amazon

Soon to be published books in the Milo Thorne series:
Culpepper Gulch
Widowmaker
Grave Measures

Made in the USA
San Bernardino,
CA

58892567R00100